J.A. Culican

H.M. Gooden

ISBN- 978-1-949621-09-9

www.dragonrealmpress.com

To our beta readers.

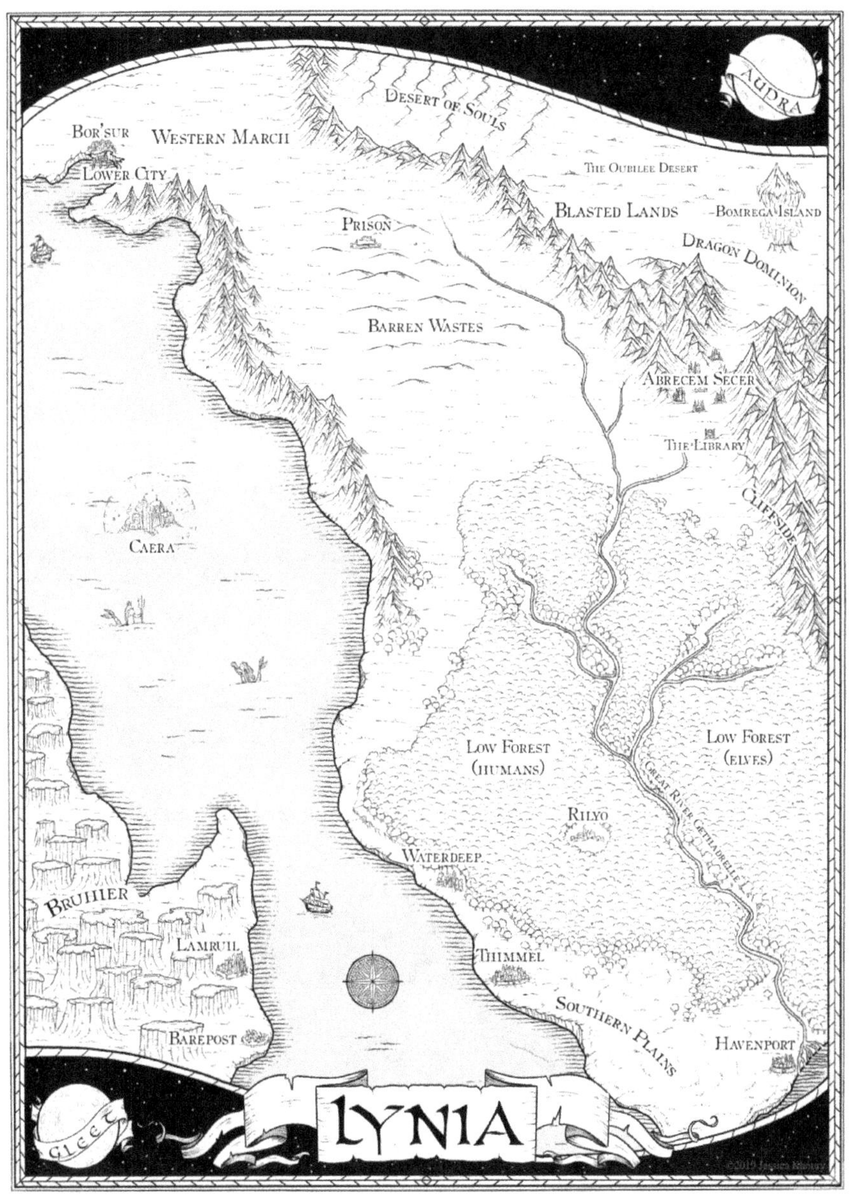
Audra
Desert of Souls
Bor'sur
Western March
Lower City
The Oubilee Desert
Blasted Lands
Bomrega Island
Prison
Dragon Dominion
Barren Wastes
Abrecem Secer
The Library
Cliffside
Caera
Low Forest
(humans)
Low Forest
(elves)
Great River Gethadrelle
Rilyo
Waterdeep
Bruhier
Lamruil
Thimmel
Southern Plains
Barepost
Havenport
Gleet
Lynia

CONTENTS

"Full speed ahead!" I called to the giants that helmed Captain Rose's ship. The wind whipped my hair hard as we flew to our destination. I held on to one of the masts to keep my balance. My heart pounded proudly at what we had just accomplished.

Stepping onto a box, I lifted my hand to my eyes, shielding them from the sun. My nerves eased as we cleared the main island after raiding an ur'gel nest. We'd lost two crew, but there were more signing up for our cause each day. We managed to keep the ur'gel at bay, but it would only be a matter of time before they found their way to the Islands. These raids bought us time while we figured out how to deal with the prison.

Captain Rose had granted me permission to use her ship in our war. She wouldn't make the crossing—it was at our own risk, which was fine by me. I had found my purpose again. To protect the Islands and fix the rip in the prison so Dag'draath could never escape. We raided the mainland shores and were able to keep the ur'gel from making a move across the water.

Once I restored the peace, I would leave quietly. I'd assume another name and live a peaceful life as a healer in some remote village where no one had heard the name Aria Trevil. I'd only tell Sade when I was ready to leave.

I held back tears. I'd leave Beru behind. My presence was a constant reminder to him of how his family was murdered. He remained in a silent sleep because of what I had put him through. His pain was so deep, he was unable to live.

I shook my head as my hand wiped away the single tear that fell down my cheek. The others couldn't see my weakness. They needed me to be a leader. With that promise, I held back any emotions that broke through to the surface. I'd deal with them later, if at all.

"Aria, we've cleared the mainland's water," one of the crew reported to me.

"Let's pick up our speed. The sooner we get back, the sooner we can feast. I want everyone to celebrate." I stepped down from the box and made my way to the wheelhouse. With my hand on the doorknob, I watched Sade perfectly maneuvering the ship. She had been a quick study of Captain Rose and commanded the ship on each crossing. She'd had to remain on the ship because we couldn't risk losing her in battle, which had been a struggle for her.

“Full steer ahead, captain.” I stood at attention and saluted her with a goofy grin.

“Oh, please. I get that enough from everyone else. Is it that hard to believe I could run this ship?” She smiled coyly and turned her attention back to the wheel.

“Of course not. But we're not going to let that stop us from teasing you.” I jumped up on the wooden dash and sat down. “It was a good raid. Even with our losses. I think they are beginning to find us a nuisance. They’ve been staying back from the coast.”

“If only all of them would follow suit. We've got to find a way to put an end to this. Before Dag’draath breaks free. It won’t be easy to fight them with him in command.”

She was right, but finding a solution proved to be more difficult than we had planned. Beru was the key, but he was barely alive, let alone conscious. We hadn't been able to come up with another plan. We needed him to wake up and be a warrior again, but that didn't look like it would happen anytime soon.

“Has he made any improvement?”

“No. Slight eye movement. A twitch here and there. There is a nurse with him when one of us is not there.”

She didn't respond, nor did she look interested in my response.

I'd leave it at that. I walked over and watched as she used a string to determine the fastest way home.

"We are here—past these few islands." She pointed out the window. "We should let them rest before our next raid. Do you think we'll have time?"

"I hope so." I left the wheelhouse and watched as the crew released the ropes to slow the ship so we could safely pull into port.

Captain Rose pulled herself up the ropes and flew over the railing with ease. "About time. I've got to move some cargo. How soon can you turn the ship over?" Captain Rose's voice was rough as she walked past me to the wheelhouse.

"Sade will hurry," I called back to her, but she had already closed the door. I flipped my legs over the side of the railing and began to climb down. It wasn't long before I heard Iri in the distance, arguing. I turned my head to see who he was talking to.

A lone priest stood before him and appeared to be trying to convince him of something.

"And why do you believe that? Just because you read it in a book?" Iri crossed his arms over his chest.

"Are you not a believer?" The priest raised his eyebrows and held both of his palms up to the sky.

“I don’t believe everything people tell me. I'm not a follower.” Iri smiled at the priest as if he were challenging him.

I climbed down the rope faster in hopes of interrupting their conversation. The last thing we needed was to draw attention to us. The ropes slipped through my fingers as my foot missed a rung. With burning hands, I ran toward the duo.

“Iri. Can I get some help?” He smiled as my voice reached him. When I came within arm's reach, he pulled me close.

“You know he is safe here. I should be able to go on the raids with you,” Iri grumbled under his breath as he looked up at the ship.

“It's not on my command you have to stay with Beru,” I reminded him. It was hard for him to watch us fight while he stayed and babysat.

“No, you’re right. But it's still not fair.” Iri followed me as we walked back to the temple.

“Any improvement today?” I asked, changing the subject.

Iri’s shoulders slumped. “No. Much the same. Astor sat with him this afternoon and tried a few spells, but nothing produced a reaction.”

I offered him a small smile and avoided saying anything else. I knew what had to happen. I needed to push past all the negative thoughts and free Beru from his new prison. The raids would not end until we were in control of the key. My mood shifted as I focused on what had to be done. So far, nothing we tried had worked. We needed to activate the beast in him.

He was a fighter to his core. If we awoke that power, he would come back to us. I had to believe that. With each step, I could feel my heartbeat pounding, ready to invoke the new power.

"Where are you going?" Iri grabbed my arm.

Determination took over. "I'm going to wake Beru."

"If you could do that, wouldn't you have done it already? I have every bit of faith in you, but I can't watch you fail at something because it's out of your control."

I knew I was the only one who could wake him. It always came back to Beru and me. "I've got to try something new. Something different from anything we have done. Nothing has worked so far. But he's in there, and he's waiting for us to free him. We can't let him down. He saw something so traumatic he has hidden himself from the world. I need him to find the fighter he is. I'm not sure how to do that quite yet, but I've got to try something." I took a deep breath.

Iri wasn't an emotional man, so I wasn't sure if he would be on board with any tactics I would be ready to use.

“Just holler if you need me.” Iri walked off to the side of the temple.

“Aria.” Someone called my name as I was about to enter the temple. My hand hovered on the doorknob, and I was tempted to ignore whoever it was. Against my better judgment, I stopped and looked back over my shoulder to see Sade run up behind me and throw a bag at me, which I deftly caught.

“What’s this?”

“Our bounty. Bad news. Just got word of a large attack on the mainland. Captain Rose has given us the go-ahead to take the ship back. The crew’s loading new supplies, and we should be ready to go soon.”

I looked back at the door and hesitated. I was finally ready to face him. To anger him enough to come back to us. If I left now, I may lose the will to do it again. I didn't have to explain it to her. She understood something was different—that I had a new plan.

“I have something I need to do first.”

“Whatever it is, just do it. Wake him up. We need to move.” She took off.

I watched her go, losing my nerve. I glanced back at the door and hesitated. I wanted to do this later, but something in the pit of my stomach screamed to do it now. We needed him. As he slept, more people would die and more battles would ensue until the prison was ripped apart.

Exhaling a harsh breath, I pushed the door open and forced myself to walk directly to his side.

He lay in the exact same position as when I left hours ago. His dark hair sprawled in a mess around his too pale face. Beru's chest rose and fell at uneven intervals as I leaned over his bed to grab his hand. My hand brushed his, which was cold to the touch.

With just a hair space between us, I gently kissed his cheek, thankful he couldn't feel my touch. It was about the only positive thing about his deep sleep. I had sat beside his bed for many nights and watched him. Memorized his face like I couldn't before.

He needed to know how the world had changed since he had fallen into his deep sleep. He couldn't sit by as innocent lives were lost. Lost because of what we had done.

My mind raced, wondering how to convince him to come back to us. To leave his own misery and help us fight and gain control again. He was the key and time was almost up for figuring out exactly what that meant and what we were going to do about it.

I threw the bounty bag that had been wrapped around my hand onto his lap. An ur'gel head rolled out of the bag and off the bed onto the floor with a clunk. “It's time to get up,” my voice whispered next to his ear.

Beru's arm swung out reflexively, barely clipping my side, and missed capturing the bounty bag completely.

"Beru, can you hear me?" I lowered myself to the edge of his bed and grabbed his arm, my fingers tangling in his shirt. My heart raced at the thought of him coming back to us. To me.

He moaned, moving his head back and forth, appearing to be caught in some sort of inner turmoil. His body stiffened and a look of pain crossed his face. Sweat poured down his cheeks as his body moved more. I panicked, uncertain what to do.

"Iri," I screamed, running toward the door.

He came barreling toward me.

"He's awake." My hands shook as I tried to say more, but my voice gave out.

He grabbed my hands in his and spoke calmly. "I'm here now. Let's go and welcome him back."

I gulped and nodded as he led me back to Beru's room. My eyes closed as we entered, afraid it was all a mistake.

"Beru?" Iri propped his heavy body over the bed and placed his hand on Beru's shoulder. "Have you come back to us?"

I remained by the door, my hands covering my mouth as I shook. I watched for any sign he was indeed awake. His foot moved under the blanket, and I couldn't stop myself from jumping up and down. I pointed to the spot for Iri. "His foot."

He lifted the blanket to see for himself. "I think you're right. He's ready."

My body felt tingly as I tried to control myself in front of Iri. All my healing knowledge was forgotten in that moment and I ignored the fact I should be preparing for his return. The butterflies in my stomach overtook any adult thoughts of healing him. I knew it wasn't his body that needed healing. It was his soul and his mind that I broke. I had no knowledge of the soul. Many healers were old souls. I never fit into that category, wanting nothing more than to be a warrior, not a healer. I blamed my parents for that, even if it was wrong.

"What should we do?" Iri turned toward me.

My mind stuttered as my first thought was to take him to Mother Ofburg. No one would go for that as she was quite far away and wasn't speaking to me. Again, something that was my fault. Yet, I knew she would put her differences aside to help him because she was a true healer. It didn't matter to her what side the person was on. She would give her all as she had given her life to healing.

"Water. We should get him water. He's very dehydrated and probably feels nauseous." I nodded repeatedly as if to convince myself I could handle the situation. Iri seemed to take the bait as he left the room in a hurry.

I immediately took his place beside the bed and held Beru's hand in mine, which was still too cold. Color returned to his face with each passing moment as he became stronger. He appeared to be struggling with the Fits. His body would stiffen out straight and his breathing was still labored. In his state, I knew if he woke, his confusion would be overwhelming. I needed him calm.

"You're okay. Just relax and let it happen naturally," I whispered in his ear as I pushed his sweat drenched hair out of his eyes. His body relaxed and his breathing regulated.

My fingers combed through his hair as I waited for Iri to return. Anxiety poured over me about being in his presence alone. The last time I had been with him was in the market with his family. Ever since that time, whenever I closed my eyes, I relived the death of his wife and the screams of his young children as the ur'gel killed them. The love he had for his family was palpable. I used that love to break him, all because I couldn't stand to lose my own brother—to see him killed. Now the prison was broken. But Beru was free and the connection we had . . .

Guilt enveloped me for comparing his feelings to my own. Beru lost his whole family. Mine was safe and alive.

Iri made his way back into the room with a pitcher of water and a glass. "You should do this part." He held the items out to me.

I took them and poured some of the water into the glass. "Can you move him back on the pillows?"

Iri moved Beru's blankets and pulled him up by the armpits so he was at a slant. "This good enough?"

"Yes, thank you." I took the cup and placed it at Beru's lips. I had to be careful not to drown him in my enthusiasm. "Open your lips if you can."

Beru parted his lips, and I slowly tipped the glass for him to take a sip. He moved his head away, and I sat back with the glass. I watched intensely as he opened his eyes for the first time. He looked around the room but didn't appear to see Iri or me. His eyes didn't focus on us or anything in the room. They were glazed over and continue to move around.

"Can you hear me?"

Iri sat down on the opposite side of the bed, and Beru's eyes followed him.

We watched Beru for any signs of recognition. Finally, his eyes drifted over to Iri, and he nodded his head. Iri slapped his hands together with a great big laugh of excitement.

“I was beginning to think I would never see the day, old chap.” Iri slapped Beru's leg a little too hard in his excitement. “I'm sorry.” Iri immediately rubbed the spot where he had hit him and then backed away.

“It's okay, he won’t break. Just be a little gentler.” I smiled at how a great warrior like Iri could be as gentle as a little kitten.

When I looked back at Beru, his eyes were focused on me. His expression was intense, and I immediately stood, backed away from the bed, and took the water to the other side of the room to place on a low dresser. My hands shook with nervousness at what Beru and I had shared the last time he was awake. I knew he would have questions, and I would be forced tell him I had purposely put us in that position. He’d hate me for it.

“Aria has been taking good care of you. We've all done our shifts, and everyone will be excited to hear you’re back.” Iri pulled up a chair and sat next to the bed.

I kept my face away from them but tilted my ear back to listen to their conversation as I grabbed a cloth and wiped down the top of the dresser. He had yet to say anything but began moaning.

"It will come with time, my friend." I heard Iri state.

I had wasted enough time pretending to wipe the dresser dry and knew it was time for me to return to Beru's side. Exhaling, I turned to find Beru's eyes on me. Pulling a chair next to his bed, I sat uneasily next to him, across from Iri. I avoided his eyes and maintained a neutral smile as I kept my hands busy monitoring his vital signs. My fingers found the pulse on his wrist and I counted to myself. I remained in that position longer than I needed to. Beru's warmth was back and I wanted to soak it in while I still could.

"I should get going. I'll let the others know about his condition." Iri stood from his chair.

"No, don't go." I shot up from my own chair, unable to hide how nervous I was. "Please stay."

I looked down at Beru, and his eyes never left me. I couldn't read his face. It was neutral, and his eyes appeared different. The color had changed. They were darker and cloudy, almost as if a film covered them

"Surely you can take care of him. Is there something else?" Iri tilted his head and scrunched up his eyebrows. I stood frozen, and Iri nodded for me to follow him out of the room.

I quickly obliged, and we walked to the foyer. Iri closed the door behind us. “What is this about? Aren't you happy he's come out of it?”

“Yes, of course I am. It's just that . . .” I didn't know the right words to say. I wasn't sure he would understand my predicament. He hadn't made the choice to break Beru and show him how his family died. Iri had no family and had only recently became attached to us.

“Well, spit it out.” Iri leaned against the wall and let out a giant sigh.

“I'm afraid he's going to hate me for what I did.” I blurted it all out quickly in hopes the boulder that sat on my chest would disappear. The guilt was suffocating me. There was no relief with my confession. I feared he would think me an evil person. That he too would be against me. My eyes focused on the knots on the wooden deck. I didn't want to see the disappointment on his face.

“You did what you had to do with the knowledge that you had. There was no way you could have known how his family was murdered.” Iri wrapped his massive arms around me, and I fell into his chest and cried. My whole body shook as I let out every emotion.

“I won't be able to accept him hating me for what I did to him. He didn't deserve that, no matter what good we were trying to do. He should have never seen that. If I’d have known, I would have never gone along with the plan." I pulled away from him and used my sleeve to wipe away my tears.

"And when he's good and ready, you can tell him that." He used the bottom of his shirt to help me wipe my face.

"I'm scared to go back in there."

"He had two hundred and fifty years of repressed emotions come flooding back to him. You're one of his closest friends. You know what his life was like in that prison, and now you know what happened to his family. You're the one person he needs right now."

"I think his wife and kids were the reason he was able to cope. But not anymore," I whispered into his shirt.

"Then you need to be the reason he's able to cope now. And I have every faith in you. There is nothing but goodness in your heart. There will always be times when you're called to do more than you think you can. This is one of those times."

He was right. I couldn't abandon Beru. I needed to put my feelings aside and help him through this dark time. It would be complicated, but I had my friends to lean on. We'd all get him through it.

"Now, I want you to go in there and be his friend. I'm going to go tell the others and then I'll be back. Don't let him slip away again."

I turned back to the door and took a deep breath. I would do it. For him, I'd make everything better. The door creaked open to reveal that Beru was more awake than when we had left him. He had propped himself up more on the pillows and drunk the full glass of water by his bedside.

“How are you doing?” I mentally chided myself for such an insensitive question.

“Sore.” His hand rubbed his stomach.

“Are you hungry? I could fetch you something.” I pointed to the doorway, eager to run back out.

“Sit.” He patted the bed beside him, his muddied eyes still trained on me.

I walked over in silence and sat down. “I’m sorry about what happened. If I’d known, I'd never have taken you.” My voice broke as I forced myself to meet his gaze.

He moaned something I couldn’t understand. I leaned in closer to hear better, and all I could make out was, “You knew.” He drifted off into the abyss again, and I grew weak, knowing I had broken the only man able to keep Dag'draath in the prison. The man who’d stolen my heart.

The noise of a loud horn filled the air. I jumped in my seat and looked at Beru, who was still sleeping soundly. I ran to the window and watched as people ran about with looks of fear on their faces. Iri ran toward the temple, and I ran out and met him in the foyer.

"What's that noise?"

We had never heard it before.

"It's the cloud network. Most people here have never heard it in use before, either." Iri walked into Beru's room. "He's back in his slumber?"

"Yes." Iri paced in front of me.

"What is the cloud network?"

"It's a series of horns that activate when the Islands are under attack." Iri stood still long enough to get the one sentence out.

"We're being attacked?" I asked in disbelief. The Islands were a safe haven, with many barriers of defense before anyone could reach them.

“Those raids must have been a distraction, so they could make their way here undetected.” Iri couldn’t stand still. “We need to get him out of here. Can we move him without hurting him further?”

“Yes, his issue is more in the soul than physical.” We both entered the room and searched for anything we could lift him with. The temple only held the necessities of their people, which meant it was rather barren.

“We may have to leave him here. They won't find him right away. Maybe Astor could make up some protection spell to keep them from entering the temple. It may be our only choice right now.” Iri looked at me for guidance.

“How much time do we have before they arrive?” I placed my hand on Beru’s forehead, making sure his warmth was still there.

“It's hard to say. We still have no idea how far up they have made it. Or who—”

Banging on the door interrupted Iri and we both involuntarily took a step back. Our eyes met as the worst passed through our minds until we heard Sade calling our names.

Snapping out of the fear, I rushed to the door to let her in.

“They're here.” She hurried past us into the temple. “Is he ready to go?” She nodded toward Beru.

"No, he's back into his slumber." I looked at the ground as if she could see through me and knew my sins.

"What do we do about him? They have to be here for him or you."

Panic built inside me. Each breath shook and my hands and feet were numb. I didn't have any answers, and I felt guilty. I had started this war. I should know what to do right now, but I was frozen in fear.

"We have to leave him here. We will leave guards at the doors and see if Astor can help in any magical way."

"I'll get Astor." Iri ran out the door, leaving us alone.

"What happened with him? I thought he was awake finally." She stepped past me and walked to Beru. She prodded him in the stomach to see if she could wake him. "That's weird. How can he be awake one moment and not the next?"

"I'm not sure." I didn't offer much to the conversation. I was confused at how the Islands were being attacked on top of worrying about Beru.

"What did he say when he was awake?" She turned to me as if I would have the answers.

I shrugged. He really hadn't spoken. Mostly moaned and seemed aware of what we were saying to him. "He was groggy. Not fully aware of what was going on. But he was awake."

“We've got to leave to fight them anyway. I'm not sure how to handle this except for the fighting part. We need to talk to Captain Rose.” She walked past me out of the room. “Have you dreamwalked since we arrived at the temple?”

“No. I'll go talk to Captain Rose. Can you stay here and wait for Iri and Astor? Make sure they don't turn him into a toad.” I forced a smile to cover my fear.

Without waiting for a reply, I left. I walked quickly down to the dock and hoped I could catch Captain Rose before she left with her cargo. I needed to focus on the new attacks, not on Beru.

The ur'gel were not used to the land, so we had that advantage over them. That was the only positive in any of it.

I caught sight of Captain Rose’s ship, still in the same place we had left it. Several of the workers were unloading some cargo from it. I waited till the last one was down and began my climb. Once on board, I searched for her. The deck was full of activity. Giants were unloading anything they could. I walked to the wheelhouse, where I thought she must be. I swung open the door and watched the fury unfold. She flung papers about as she looked through drawers with urgency.

“It's here somewhere,” she muttered as she rifled through papers and maps.

“Can I help you find something?”

She pointed her finger at me. “You're the reason they're here.”

“I know. I've come to speak to you about it. I need you to take us to the mainland. I need to go back to my village. They want Beru. I must wake him from his slumber and get him back to what he used to be. There’s only one person who can help me do that.” I tried to sound as convincing as possible because she had stated before she did not go to the mainland.

“That's impossible. No one has flown over the mainland. It's just not possible.”

“Why is that? What's to stop you from flying over the mainland?” I didn't want to sound harsh, but she had never given us a reason why it was not possible. Nobody had ever flown there, so there must be a reason why.

“It’s just not possible. No one does it.” She continued to dig through the wheelhouse.

I ducked as she threw a book backward from the drawer she was digging in. It slammed against the wall next to my head.

She muttered about “it” being in here.

“What are you looking for? Maybe I can help,” I offered as I stepped closer to her.

"An old map of the Islands. There are some secret tunnels . . ." She stopped when she realized what she'd disclosed and looked back at me, wagging her stubby finger. "You better not say anything."

"Your secret is safe with me." I held my hands up in a sign of submission.

Her worried look seemed to ease, and she got back to digging through drawers. "There are tunnels we can guide people to. That should keep them safe until we get rid of the enemy."

"What does it look like?" I began digging through the mess of papers on the floor.

"It's fragile," she piped up, and I glanced around the room at everything thrown about. "Green paper if I recall."

I started in the farthest corner and made my way toward her. "So, you're not interested in going over the mainland? To see if it's possible?" I baited her ego. She was a forward thinker and being the first to do something would be her thing.

"Nope. I'll stop you there. I like you, kid, but there are some things we can't test. Shouldn't test. And this is one of them." She stood up and stretched, placing her hands on her back. "I'll drop you off at the mainland. That's about all I can do."

I nodded and accepted defeat. As I looked down, I noticed a small piece of green sticking out from a book. I grabbed it. “Is this it?”

“Holy Dickins! It is.” Captain Rose grabbed the paper from my hand and spread it out on the table to get a good look at it. “I don’t know if they have been covered or not, but it’s something to start with.

“Can you take us to the mainland before you go to the caves?” I was ready to plead with her. We needed to stop the ur’gel from attacking and get Beru back to being himself as soon as possible.

“This journey will stop them from attacking us?” she questioned as she unfolded the paper.

“I believe so. If I’m right, they know Beru is the Key, and they want him. If we get him better, we can make a go for it.” I started to pick up items on the floor.

“Leave that. I’ll take you now. Round up whoever is coming. I’ll get rid of this mess. Bring Beru with you. I’ll send help to carry him onboard.”

I nodded. I had preferred to leave him but would take any help she offered.

We loaded the ship and recruited a few crew members to carry on with us to my village. Beru had come around in the salt air and was in and out of his slumber. Captain Rose was sure that was a good sign he was on the mend.

We left port, and it wasn't long before we could hear the ur'gel attacking below. We could see they were at the cliffs as they fought their way to the city. The screams of the slaughter with the Cloud Network Horns was deafening. My nerves itched with the need to stay and fight but leaving was the best way to protect everyone.

"It's different running away from it when you're used to running toward it." Sade's voice came from over my shoulder.

We both watched helplessly as the ur'gel seemed to get the better of the giants. There were too many of them. It was only a matter of time before they reached the cities. Captain Rose had left the map with the tunnel locations with a local, and they started the evacuations of the civilians.

"I hope it's the same as we left it when we return." I leaned over the edge to get a better view as we flew by. Some of the ur'gel watched in amazement as they had never seen flying ships, much like we hadn't when we'd arrived.

"I wonder if Widow is down there." She propped herself up and searched the crowd as we flew by. "She'd probably string a web to the ship if she was."

I was quiet, deep in thought about my plan. I knew it was time to tell her where we were going. "I'm going to take him to Mother Ofburg. I'm going to ask her to help us get him back."

She flipped her head in my direction, and her jaw dropped. Time went on as she just stared at me and didn't speak. I gave her time to process. As we cleared the last island, a rainbow appeared off in the distance. I took it as a sign this was the right decision.

"You're taking a big chance. Did you forget how the last couple of times went when you saw her? She's not your fan anymore." She seemed to have tried to choose her words wisely.

"I've not forgotten. But she's a healer at her core. She won't refuse him. If there is anyone who can make him whole again, it's her. I'd bet my life on it." I breathed in the salty air and felt relaxed for the first time in a while.

"You are betting your life, I'm afraid."

"Are you with me on this, even though you don't agree? I need your support for it to work."

"I'm always with you. No matter what crazy shit you want to do." She leaned her body in and bumped my shoulder.

I smiled at her loyalty, even though I didn't believe I deserved it. She had become like a sister to me, and I didn't want to let her down. I shivered, even though I was warm. It *was* a possibility Mother Ofburg would shut the door in my face again.

"There's no way you'll make it here," Captain Rose observed as we reached the mainland's shores. The beaches were lined with ur'gel. They raised their weapons and yelled up at the ship as we hovered closer to them.

"Can you take us in further?" My eyes pleaded desperately with her. She couldn't take us back now. She had to take us farther.

Captain Rose didn't respond. She watched the ur'gel and navigated around the beach. There was no place safe to land, and we couldn't risk the ur'gel taking over her ship. I left my question to sit with her, each moment that passed more certain she would take us farther inland.

Sade entered the wheelhouse with a frown. "There's no way to land here. It's a death wish." She slammed the door behind her.

"I'll try for the nearest clearing. That's the best I can do." Captain Rose shook her head.

"Thank you." I wanted to run up and hug her, but I figured she would deck me, so I hid my smile.

“There are a few places I can think of.” Sade walked over to the maps.

“You won’t find any there. Like I said, we don’t cross the mainland.” Captain Rose forged ahead and increased the speed of the ship as we flew over the ur’gel. “Just let me clear these creatures first. Hang on.”

I gripped a rail as the boat jetted ahead with a jolt. I cranked my head toward the window, afraid we had lost someone overboard.

Captain Rose let out a large, bellowing laugh. “Your faces were priceless.”

Sade raised one eyebrow at me, not amused at the captain’s ramblings.

As soon as we flew over the beach, headed into the forest, and cleared the ur’gel, Captain Rose slowed the ship back to average speed. We were able to walk around the wheelhouse and deck again without risk of falling.

“I’ll check on Beru,” I told them as they began to chat about where we could land.

I slipped out of the wheelhouse and walked across the deck. The creatures and crew were putting things back into place after they had been thrown about. They were securing them with rope this time, which made me wonder if it wasn’t a standard Captain Rose maneuver.

I opened the door on the opposite side of the wheelhouse where Iri, Astor, and Beru were staying. It was Captain Rose's bunkhouse. I walked inside to find Beru sitting up in bed with Iri on a chair next to him and Astor on the bunk above him.

"Everyone all right in here?"

They all had serious looks on their faces, and I wondered what they had been talking about.

"As fine as we could be. We saw the ur'gel on the beach. We assumed that was the reason for the ship's crazy movements." Iri took a drink from his cup.

"Yes, she was afraid of them attacking the ship. They are looking for a place where we can land, farther away from them. Inland." I took the seat farthest from Beru, where Iri blocked my view of him.

The ship suddenly felt like it jumped, and our bags fell from one of the bunks onto the floor. Iri placed both hands on the walls to steady himself. He didn't like flying ships. It wasn't water in his cup.

"It's turbulence. We're okay," I reassured him, planting my feet firmly on the wall and floor to steady myself from any more sudden movements. "How is he?"

"You should ask him yourself." Iri smiled and moved back so I could see Beru. He looked handsome in the candlelight, his white shirt against his dark tanned skin. I was happy for the dimness in the room—it made me more at ease.

"How are you feeling?" I hoped he would answer more clearly than before. I'd tried to make sense of what he had said to me before he fell back to sleep, but it was impossible. Instead, it filled me with worry.

"Living." One side of his mouth tilted up. He looked comfortable against the pillow.

"Better than the alternative," I joked timidly. He would know something was up with me. I couldn't get it together in front of him. I hoped Iri or Astor would interject and kill the awkwardness that had filled the room when I entered.

Beru's eyes were trained on me. I met them, and we shared a moment. An acknowledgment of what we had seen in the village. I glanced away quickly to dull his pain. I stood up just as we hit another current, and my head knocked against the side of the wall with a thud.

I shook my head and found myself on the ground as the last of the blackness faded away. I must have lost consciousness for a few moments. Iri was by my side, and Beru was sitting sideways on his bed. Astor jumped down from his bunk and helped Iri bring me over to an empty bottom bunk.

"Lie here for a while." Iri propped my head up with another pillow.

I closed my eyes, seeing double of everything.

"How is she doing?" Beru said from across the room.

"Just a bump, but we shouldn't let her fall asleep. I remember her saying that once," Astor chimed in.

I couldn't help but break into a smile. I opened my eyes to see their concerned faces staring back at me, glad to be seeing only one of each of them. "I'll be fine. I just need to rest for a few minutes."

"I'm going up to see what's going on with Captain Rose." Iri stood and flexed his shoulders.

"No." I reached over and tried to grab his hand, but my head began to spin the moment I sat up, causing me to almost topple out of the bunk.

"Lie down." Astor gently placed me back on the pillow. "You have to give yourself some time."

"I'll be back." Iri opened the door and left.

"I'm going with him. I have to keep him in line." Astor winked at me.

"Um . . . no, please stay." I grabbed onto his arm for dear life as he went to leave. He couldn't leave me alone with Beru.

"Just rest." Astor looked over at Beru and then back at me and winked. "He's all yours," he whispered, much to my horror. I prayed Beru hadn't heard him.

Astor made his getaway before there was anything I could do. There we were—Beru and I—alone again.

"You sure you're fine over there?" I heard him grunt as he moved.

"Yes, just a little dizzy." I placed my hand over my eyes. At least he wasn't on the bunk next to me. I almost breathed a loud sigh of relief but stopped myself.

"You'll have a big bruise. You hit the wall pretty hard." I heard him as he moved. Was he coming over?

I lifted my hand a little until I had him in sight. He had flipped his legs over the side of his bunk and was trying to stand up. My heart raced, and I panicked. I looked back toward the door and wondered if I could make a run for it. *Stop! You're crazy. Just breathe.*

I heard his footsteps as he came closer and the bottom of his cane as it hit the floor. He heaved his body into the bottom bunk across from me. There was no candle in the bunk, so I couldn't see if he was watching me.

"You've crossed leaps and bounds. You were barely awake when they carried you onboard." I lifted my hand and tried to get a better look at him.

"You sound disappointed." He chuckled and got comfortable in the bed.

"No, I didn't mean . . ."

"I know." He let out a moan as he settled in. I didn't hear any movement after that.

"I'm sorry."

"I don't want to talk about it," he interrupted me again. "Maybe later, but not now."

The boat slammed against another current and almost turned sideways. We both held onto our bunk posts.

"That Captain Rose may need some flying lessons." Beru helped straighten us out.

"It's the current from the wind in the trees. She must be taking us farther inland." I kept one hand on the bunk rail and my foot on the wall.

"She's breaking her own rule, then." Beru lit his candle and was in full view again.

"Not because she wants to. The beach was full of ur'gel." I turned on my side to face him, pulling the blanket out from under me so I could cover up in it to feel more secure.

His eyes never came my way. He lay on his back, hands behind his head.

I rested my head on my hands and waited for him to speak again. My nerves had fallen away once he'd declared he didn't want to talk about what happened in the village.

The ship pulled to a full stop, and we both hit the heads of the bunks and then fell on the floor on top of each other. Pain filled my body as I fought gravity to pull myself up.

Beru reached for my arm to steady me and I fell into his lap.

"We may be safer down here." He smiled up at me.

I thought I would melt. It had been too long since I had seen that smile. It almost felt like old times. As if there wasn't any awkwardness around us anymore.

The door opened, and Sade and Iri stood there frozen as if they had just walked in on a private moment between us.

"Should we leave?" She pointed toward the door.

"No. We fell out of the bunk. We each had our own bunk," I added to avoid any confusion they may have. Iri helped me up first, and I sat in my bunk. Then they lifted Beru up into his bunk.

"What's going on out there?" Beru settled back in.

"The ship can't get enough height over the trees. We have a clearing in mind, but we haven't found a way to get to it yet." Sade propped up his feet with a pillow.

"The winds are too strong. They keep pulling us into currents. If we can't reach the clearing soon, Captain Rose is going to turn back around." She sat next to me.

"Where do we want to be?" Beru looked at each of our faces. Iri and Sade looked back at me.

"We were seeking help for you. To bring you back from wherever you were." I watched as he half smiled and then turned away from us. I felt his pain but didn't understand his worry.

He had loved so deeply before and lost it. I would never understand that.

The door opened, and Captain Rose appeared. "It's now or never. They've likely spotted the ship now that we have stopped and are on their way. Best get a move on."

I stood and grabbed my bag, and the others followed. Beru stayed seated. "I'm afraid I'm the tagalong."

"We have recruits who have signed on to help. They will get you down the rope." I placed my hand on his and hoped I lessened his worry.

"I'll manage. I'm sore, but I feel strong." He put his other hand on top of mine and squeezed.

I tried to move, but he held on longer. There were so many unspoken things between us.

"Let's go," Sade called.

I looked around the room and noticed the others had left already. I pulled him up. The force propelled his body toward mine.

His breath fell softly on my cheeks and warmed them. "Ready?"

I looked into his eyes and nodded.

His attention to me was different. More heated. Unresolved.

"Can we do this romance shit later?" Sade's head was slightly turned, and her hands were on her hips. "We're kinda in a life and death situation right now."

We made our way on deck, and Iri and Astor were already on their way down. Two giants took Beru, even though he wanted to go alone. Sade went over next. I went last.

As soon as my feet were on the ground, Captain Rose pulled the ropes up, and they were on their way back to the Islands. We had only what we could carry and needed to get supplies before we left for the village.

"How much time do you think we have?" Sade threw two packs over her back.

"Not much." Beru pointed to the woods.

We heard the cracking of branches that indicated someone walked amongst them. I waved my arm to get everyone's attention and motioned for them to follow me before we were made.

We escaped without incident and found our way to a small town. We all stood shocked because the raids appeared not to have affected it. People walked about doing their regular business as if the ur'gel weren't attacking communities at random.

"Why do I feel like I just stepped into another world?" Sade squinted. "It's as if they have no idea about the battle happening around them."

The storefronts boasted fruits and vegetables and displayed them along the sidewalk. Women carried their full baskets in preparation for that evening's supper. No one looked up fearfully at the strangers who entered their town. They didn't appear to even notice us.

"Let's get our supplies and move on," Iri suggested. "Something's not right here."

We agreed to split up and separate the tasks. Sade and I would get food and Iri and Astor would look for lodging and try to secure some horses and a carriage for us. Beru would stay behind with the two giants and rest until we met back up shortly.

Sade and I took off in the direction of the large fruit stand. It wasn't long before she was drilling me with questions about Beru. "So, what was that, anyway?" She looked back to make sure no one was behind us. The look on her face told me she wanted all the dirt.

"Nothing happened. You walked in on an awkward moment. We both fell on the ground when the ship stopped suddenly. There's nothing more to tell." I picked up some fruit and began to fill a basket.

"It didn't look that innocent." She followed, loading up her basket.

"Well, it was. I was just embarrassed it happened and probably had a goofy look on my face." I noticed a woman not far from us who appeared to be eavesdropping on our conversation. I tried to get Sade's attention, but she was far too interested in the food. We hadn't eaten most of the fruits available since we'd left for the Islands.

"I think we have enough for the week." I nudged her arm and nodded toward the woman, who had moved away from us. "She was quite interested in our conversation."

"About unrequited love? I'm sure there are more interesting things for her to eavesdrop on." Sade's eyebrow rose.

"It's the best time of the year for these apples. They make wonderful pies." The local merchant woman filled one of the barrels with more apples.

"We aren't much for cooking." Sade took a big bite out of one of the apples. "But you're right, these are great." She grabbed two more handfuls of apples and placed them in her basket, which was quite a feat since it was filled to the brim.

The woman leaned in to whisper, "There are older ones out back that sell for a song."

"Thank you." I nodded in appreciation, but money was not a concern for us.

She walked away, and we picked through the produce. Something was odd about her.

"What do you think she meant by out back?" I watched as she greeted customers in the store.

"Behind the store? Are you part of The Council Three now?" Sade shook her head at my challenging behavior. "Maybe she was just nice."

It was a change from normal. I was the one who could see the good in people, while she was the skeptic. I kept my eyes on the woman as she walked around her store, uneasy with something about her. I tried to let it go but I just couldn't. Maybe it was the dreamwalker in me.

“Let's convince her to run away with us so she can make us apple pies.” Sade nudged my arm, proud of her joke.

“Or we could just pay for this and move on.” I smiled and she only rolled her eyes at me for blocking her joke.

I left her and entered the shop, looking for the woman so I could pay. For a small town, the store was packed. It felt like everyone who lived there was present. Something just seemed off, but I couldn't put my finger on it. Why weren’t these people afraid?

“I just saw the pie lady give away free vanilla beans. Something must be done to stop her.” Sade startled me as she leaned in from behind me to whisper.

I turned around and gave her one of my annoyed looks. I found the pay lady and gave her coin for all our groceries. As we left the store, the apple pie lady stood at the back of the store and watched us.

We walked back to where Beru and the two giants were waiting for us. I scanned the crowd, uneasy with how everyone was acting. I could see Iri and Astor were not back yet. While they hadn’t been gone long, it made me uncomfortable.

“I'm starving. I hope no one minds I'm already digging in.” Beru dug through the baskets and grabbed some carrots and apples.

“Eat what you like.” I offered food to both guards as well. I looked around the storefronts and hoped to find a pub where we could get some hot food for supper. We were all exhausted and cooking outside was not something I was looking forward to.

We all had a little snack as we waited for the boys to come back with horses and hopefully a carriage. Beru would not be strong enough to ride on a horse on his own no matter what he thought.

It began to get later in the day, and the boys had not yet returned. I started to get worried but didn’t let on to the others.

“I hope they get back soon. I'd like to get a hot plate in before it's too late. This town isn't that big. I hope they aren't already eating without us.” Sade pouted.

“They wouldn't do that. They would wait for us.”

“Unless they thought we already ate.”

“They're coming now.” Beru walked out past us.

I followed his gaze, and sure enough, Astor and Iri had just come across the street with three horses and a wagon. They smiled ear-to-ear as they approached us.

“It's about time,” Sade called out.

“Good things require patience,” Astor countered.

I just shook my head. Sometimes, I felt like I was looking after children.

“We have come back with some news. You were right to wonder why this town has carried on as if nothing is happening around it.” Iri tied the horses up and lowered the wagon door, so we could throw our packs and the food in it.

“Somebody spoke to you about it?” I was intrigued anyone would comment.

“Several people told us the same story. It seems the ur'gel have been leaving the small towns alone and attacking the bigger cities. No one has seen any spiders around here, and there have been no deaths from her poison.” Iri grabbed an apple from the barrel.

I felt uneasy with the news. Why had the towns been left out of the raids? That didn't seem to be a good enough reason. It was possible the townspeople could come together and fight against them. Why wouldn't they try to wipe them out as they moved across the land?

“That seems like an unusual attack plan. They must need the towns for some purpose.” Beru hoisted himself onto the back of the wagon.

I agreed but kept my opinion to myself. I didn’t want to feed into the fear that was settling into our group. My mind raced for any perfectly good reason for them to do this. What benefit would they have by leaving small town's alone except for supplies? But they would have taken the supplies, and this town had a bountiful amount of them. And why weren't the people from the cities that were attacked here, living peacefully?

"It doesn't make sense to me either. But you can bet there is a reason for it." Iri sat down to eat his snack, but his eyes never rested.

"Lots of people spoke to us. They all seemed happy and aware of what was going on in the cities. None of them appeared to fear it happening here," Astor added.

"I'd be scared." I shook my head in disbelief. Something needed to be uncovered. I wasn't sure we would find out before we left, but we needed to talk to more people. Someone had to fear their town may be attacked at any time.

"I wouldn't." Sade was most disagreeable lately. I wondered why. It seemed she was just disagreeing with me to disagree. I didn't bother to question her. I didn't want the townspeople hearing our conversation, but a talk was due when we were alone.

"Let's just keep our eyes open. This is the first town we reached. Let's see what the others have in store. Someone will eventually talk." Iri ate every bit of his apple.

"You know there is cyanide in apple seeds." Sade watched him lick his fingers.

"Interesting fact for you to know."

"Well, you never know when you'll need it."

Their conversation drowned out of my head, as I focused on the storefront with the merchant woman. She was standing out front watching us, her arms crossed and a stern look on her face. What was her issue? As she noticed me, she turned to talk to one of the customers. Something was not right there, but we didn't have time to figure it out.

I turned my head a little and listened to the light conversation between Sade and Iri as they talked about foods that would kill you. Sade seemed to take immense pride in her knowledge, and he found it entertaining. For a moment, I thought about the two of them—how close they were when he almost died. That closeness was no longer there, and I wondered what had happened between them. It wasn't my business, but the two of them together always seemed right to me.

"You look deep in thought." Beru sat down next to me.

"Just thinking about our next step." I kept my head straight, still unable to look at him. Every time I looked into his eyes, I was back in the village as I tried to get him to look away. I shook my head and forced the thoughts out. I wasn't helping him get over it by dwelling on it myself. "How are you feeling?"

“Getting used to this vastly different world. I don’t quite feel like myself anymore.” He picked up a rock and rubbed his thumb over the smooth side.

“Give yourself time.” I turned to offer a smile of encouragement, but his attention was on the rock. I watched how intense his gaze was and wondered what he was really thinking.

“What did you say?” He glanced over at me and caught my eyes wandering over his body.

I turned away quickly, but not fast enough. “Nothing.”

“This town is too quiet. It’s not right.” He threw the rock down and stretched out his back.

“I don’t think we will find out why before we leave, though.” I stretched out my legs and rubbed my knees.

“It’s the calm before the storm.” His eyes were focused on something in the distance, and he appeared to be in a daze.

“What do you mean?” I tried to see what had his attention so strongly.

“Something big is coming, and Dag’draath is behind it.” His voice almost sounded automated, like it wasn’t him talking.

“How do you know?” I debated shaking him to loosen the hold of whatever had taken him over.

"He'll coax you into the open." Beru turned to me, his eyes different.

I had stared into them enough to know it wasn't him. Was this part of his gift being the key? Was it a warning? I couldn't find the right words. I took note of his warning as I glanced back at my crew. I needed to protect them from Dag'draath.

"There are no children here. Have you seen any children?" Sade looked at all the people passing by us on the sidewalk.

I turned around and looked up both sides of the street. She was right. No children were playing or running around. What a curious thought. Where could they all be?

"That's fine with me." Astor laughed. "I've never known the need for people to have those greedy little creatures."

"You know you were once a child." Sade rolled her eyes at his comment.

Leave it to Astor to have an unpopular opinion. I smiled and wondered if he said such things to get everyone going. I half expected him to wink at me.

"It *is* peculiar." Iri weighed in. "They must be in school perhaps?"

"Maybe, but we should have seen one by now." We had been there most of the day and I was annoyed with myself that I hadn't noticed before she suggested it.

“Let’s ask them.” Iri walked over to someone on the side of the street while we stayed back.

As we waited for him to return, I looked at Beru, who had been keeping to himself since we last spoke. He looked deep in thought and wasn’t paying attention to our conversation.

I turned my attention back to Iri. He had moved on to another person, and they seemed to ignore him as they went.

“That’s not friendly or happy.”

Iri approached person after person, but none stopped to talk to him other than a typical greeting.

“Maybe it’s his stature. He is rather large,” Astor suggested. “Can we eat now? I’m about to pass out. Can this missing child thing wait?”

“No, it cannot wait.” My tone showed my annoyance with him.

Astor loved to be the fool of the group, but his antics had a place and a time.

“He’s coming back now,” I warned the group.

We anxiously waited for him to return to us. His face was grim. His tall body hung forward in a slump.

“Have you solved the mystery?” Astor called out to him, his motivation being food.

Iri didn't comment and waited until he was upon us. "Everyone was friendly until I asked about the children. Then, no one had time to talk to me." He shook his head.

"Happy, friendly people without children? Seems sane to me. Let's go eat now." Astor tried to pull us in the direction of the local pub.

"What did they say when you asked?" I demanded, mostly out of frustration with Astor's attitude.

"That they were busy and didn't have time to talk. They all said the exact same thing." Iri scratched his head and turned back to the road. "I don't understand it. It's like they were reading some sort of script."

I wasn't sure if Dag'draath was behind this or not, but something was amiss.

"Let's ask Ms. Apple Pie." Sade walked past me to the storefront.

As I watched her leave, my eyes drifted back to the store, and the lady was standing outside again, staring at us. She turned to leave when she saw Sade walking toward her.

Something was definitely wrong, and I had a feeling Sade had it right with the shop owner. I took off in a slow jog to meet up with her.

"Be careful, she may offer us a pie." Sade chuckled.

"You can't still be joking about this. There's too much going on for something not to be happening here." I almost fumed at how she was acting. Was she purposely trying to get under my skin? And if so, why?

"Just let me do the talking. You're too intense." She opened the door and walked over to the lady, who was standing at the back of the store.

She turned to us and looked surprised as we continued to approach her. "Can I help you, girls?" She turned on a smile that had previously not been there.

"Yes. We were wondering if you had any more of those apples you mentioned before." Sade smiled at her sweetly and then turned to me and raised her eyebrow.

"There are some out front in the bins." She smiled and then turned her back on us.

"No, the other applies." Sade tapped on her shoulder, and she turned back toward us.

"I'm afraid I don't follow you. There are apples out front." She pointed to the front door and then went back to sorting goods.

"Why are there no children here?" she blurted out to the back of the woman.

"Excuse me?" The lady appeared to be confused at the easy question as she looked over her shoulder at us.

I sighed at Sade's blunt approach. Any real chance of the woman talking was now gone. She was turned off by the questions. "She means it's curious we haven't seen any children out playing." I smiled at the woman and tried to appear as charming as I could.

"I don't know what you mean. There are children here. I can't say where they all are on your short visit here. I must get back to work. If there is anything else you need, please see the pay lady behind the desk." This time, the woman left through a door in the back.

"That doesn't sound fishy at all." Sade turned to leave the store.

I followed her out and noticed everyone in the store watching us. They all had a somber look to them, as if we were strangers there to hurt them or take something away from them.

"I'm going to find out what's going on here," Sade proclaimed as we made our way back to the men.

"And how do you propose to do that?" I ran to keep up with her longer stride.

"I don't know yet." She stopped suddenly, and I almost toppled over her. "Someone will tell us. We just have to find them."

"Any luck?" Iri walked out to meet us.

"No. Just more questions." I looked around. The townspeople were all watching us. They weren't the happy-go-lucky people we'd found when we arrived.

"Let's head to the pub. Loose lips talk." Iri waved the rest of our party over to where we were standing in the road.

We walked along the boardwalk, and people moved out of the way as we approached. Some even crossed the road. All avoided eye contact. I guessed they feared we may stop them to talk. It was odd.

"There's a pub just past that horse stand." Astor pointed ahead of us.

"I hope we are welcomed there," I mumbled as I glanced at the townsfolk around us.

"We're close to finding out." Astor marched ahead of us, and we followed in silence.

I looked over my shoulder toward Beru, who kept to the back of our little pack. A somber mood vibrated off him as he kicked at the boards beneath his feet.

We filed into the pub and were greeted warmly by the barmaid. She took us to the back of the pub and seated us at a booth, which was entirely private from the rest of the eatery. She handed us the menus and excused herself.

"As far away from everyone as we could be." Sade stewed in her seat.

I turned my attention to my crew. Each of them was looking at the menu in front of them.

"I have the urge to get her to test whatever they bring out." Sade looked around for the barmaid.

"I'm sure it will be fine." I looked at my menu.

"Yeah, we aren't children, so we'll be fine." Astor didn't look up.

The barmaid returned with a tray full of water. "This should start you all off. Shall I bring out our best wine?"

"Yes, please!" Astor was the first to speak up.

"And what can I get you all to eat?" The girl twirled at her long blonde hair as she spoke.

Everyone spoke at once, hungry from our eventful day.

The barmaid leaned over and grabbed my menu from my hand. "Act normal." She smiled. "Everything is great, and I'm telling you what's on the menu."

I nodded and tried to get everyone else's attention as they gabbed and talked about food.

"Meet me out back when I bring the next round of water. Stop asking questions." She placed my water in front of me. "Don't give anyone reason to follow you when you leave."

She continued around the table and took everyone's orders.

I looked at Iri, who was sitting on my right side, but he didn't appear to have heard her warning. My left side was open to the room. Sade sat across from me, and she was looking at me. She must have heard the barmaid.

"I'll be right back with your orders." The barmaid smiled and left us.

"What was that about? What did she say?" Sade questioned me as soon as the waitress left the table.

"She said to stop asking questions and act normal. She'll meet us out back on her cue." I made sure my voice was directed toward the table.

"Do we trust her?" Iri leaned in and spoke low in my ear.

"Who else do we have? It's the first acknowledgment that something is wrong here." I took a drink of my water and smiled in case anyone was watching us.

"We can't all leave the table." Sade followed my lead and drank from her glass.

I looked around at our group. She was right. I had to keep what the barmaid said between us three.

"Just us three. The others will stay behind." I nodded in their direction.

They talked amongst themselves, and Astor was being a clown again with the full attention of the giants. Their booming laughter echoed through the bar.

Beru had his hands around his glass with his head down, still in some kind of daze. I feared the activity of the day had worn him down.

“Agreed. What’s the cue?” Iri leaned in again, so the others would not hear.

“The next round of water. The back door is behind Sade, so we shouldn’t be too noticeable when we get up to leave.” I kept my head down, so no one could read my lips.

“And here you are.” The barmaid and two other girls carried our food to us. She placed mugs full of wine with each plate. “Anything else I can grab for you?”

“This is good. Thank you.” I smiled up at her.

She acted like she had never spoken to me other than to take my order.

I watched as they walked away from us and then dug into my food. I didn’t know when she would bring back water, and I was hungry, so I wanted to be finished before she returned.

The barmaid finally set water down on our table. “Is there anything else I can do before I take my break?”

We all mumbled no as most of the group was still working on the large portions the pub served.

"I'll be back soon, then." The barmaid walked to the exit door just off to the side of our booth and made eye contact with me.

I watched as she left and waited a couple of minutes to ward off any suspicions. "Ready?" I slipped out first and waited off to the side. We were hidden from the rest of the bar.

Sade followed and then Iri. Once they were behind me, I opened the door, and we all walked out cautiously. I wasn't sure if it would be some sort of set-up.

"Over here." The barmaid waved us over to the side where a smoking tent was set up.

We made the short run in seconds.

"What's this about?" I pulled my hood down.

"I don't have much time. They will be looking for me. You've been asking around town about the children?" The barmaid looked behind us several times, and it made me uncomfortable.

"Yes. We noticed the lack of them." Sade shivered from the cold.

"They were taken. By the ur'gel. They are being held hostage, and we must do whatever they ask of us." Her eyes were wide with fear.

I looked toward Sade and Iri, and none of us could speak. This was low, even for the ur'gel.

"What are they doing with them?" I managed to ask.

"I don't know. But we are to sacrifice one person each night or else they will kill one child. I had to warn you because they usually pick travelers."

"But by warning us, they will pick a townsperson." Sade was quick to pipe up.

"That's our problem. I know who you are. You're the only ones who can save us. I must go back before they look for me. Please wait here for a few minutes." The barmaid left before we could ask any more questions.

"We need to free the people." I paced back and forth once we were back at camp. We had waited to tell the others until we left the pub.

"We don't have time to do anything. We should pack up and leave now. This isn't our fight." Sade surprised me with her comments.

"How can you say that? They're not equipped to fight anyone." I had no idea what her problem was, but I couldn't let her talk the rest of our crew out of protecting the townspeople.

"Let's put it to a vote, then."

"Fine. Who wants to protect the innocent?" My gaze turned to each face in our group.

They looked back at me and hesitantly raised their hands.

"We stay and fight." I raised an eyebrow at Sade, willing her to deny what was right.

“They're all too scared to say no to you.” Sade turned her back to me and begin packing the camp.

“What are you doing?” I was shocked she had disobeyed what everyone wanted.

“I'm packing up the camp because we are leaving. We are all here for you, but we aren't at your disposal,” she yelled over her shoulder.

“Okay, so what is it? Why are you so mad at me? What did I do?” I had no choice but to have the conversation. I had wanted to wait until the pressure was off, but it needed to end.

Astor dragged out a chair and placed it between us. “Don't stop on my account.” His head moved between us.

“Go to bed,” I ordered him

“Stay where you are.” Sade stood with her hands on her hips. “You can't order everyone around.”

I stood there in disbelief as I looked at my friend and didn't recognize her. My mind raced with what I could have possibly done. She was always game for anything. “What did I do?”

“Ladies, that's enough. This isn't the time or the place. We have all been through a lot and are living in tight quarters. We are all friends here. Let's not forget that. It’s time for us to get some sleep.” Iri held his hands up as he approached us.

I looked over at Sade, who hadn't moved and was still staring at me. I gave in and moved first. I walked over to my bed and lay down. I heard them talking in hushed tones, but I couldn't make out what they were saying. They moved over to the camp and lay in their beds.

Her words stung. It seemed to be another thing going wrong in my life. Another person shunning me who I cared about immensely. I rolled over onto my side, away from her. Tears were trying to fall, and I couldn't let her see them.

"Are you all right?" Beru searched me for answers as I faced him.

"I thought you would be asleep." I wiped my eyes, embarrassed he had seen me in a weak moment. The last thing he needed was to worry about me.

"I can't stop thinking about the barmaid and what she told you." He handed me a handkerchief. "Take it."

"Do you think I'm controlling?" I might as well get his opinion since he must have heard her accusations.

"I think she is tired. You have also stepped into her leadership role. That can't be easy for her." He moved his hands to rest his head on them.

Perhaps he was right. I had looked up to her and relied on her guidance, and slowly, I had filled that role. I needed her less and less. Especially on the raids from the

Islands. Sade had remained on the ship as captain while I led our team to fight.

"Just let her be. Maybe throw some responsibility her way," Beru added.

I nodded in agreement. How could I not have seen that? She had given up her life as a lone wolf to join my tribe. "I'll do that. If she'll take it. Maybe when we free the townspeople."

"I have to ask you to let this town be." He sat up and rested his legs over the side of the bed.

"Not you too." I moaned and rolled over onto my back. I knew we could help them, and it wouldn't take much. The ur'gel had to be stopped, and it wasn't like we hadn't done it what felt like a million times already. Why was everyone fighting me on it?

"I know who they are up against. It won't be a battle easily won, and we can't afford to lose anyone. We must keep focused on the prison." He sounded convincing, but I'd need to know what he knew to make that decision.

"You say who. It's a certain person?" I tried to pull as much information out of him as I could.

"Yes." He lay back in his bed, his face turned away.

"Who?" I sat up, ready to sit on his bed to see his eyes. I needed to know how he really felt and who the person was.

"His name is Vinug."

I waited for him to say more, but he remained silent. I searched that name in my head for any reference in any conversation I had ever had before, and nothing came up. Beru had never mentioned him to me before.

"How do you know him?" I'd start easy with my questions.

"I'll tell you more in the morning. It's too dark to tell if we are being watched." He rolled over onto his side, away from me.

"You promise?"

"Yes."

I lay on my back, annoyed at waiting. I wanted him to tell me everything about Vinug right away, but I would have to be patient because he did have a point about the darkness around us. I moved to my side and watched him sleep, his silhouette barely outlined by the moons.

The sun beating down on my face woke me up the next morning. I jolted upright and looked toward Beru's bed. It was empty. I could smell food cooking on the campfire and heard chatter. I hurried to get ready for the day and noticed I was the only one still sleeping. I cursed myself and my abilities for sleeping in. Even Astor was awake.

I practically ran toward the campfire, nervous Beru had told the others about Vinug, and I was the only person who didn't know what was happening.

"The sleeping beauty awakes!" Astor stood up and removed his hat as he saluted me.

"I'm sorry. I must have been more tired than I thought." I took the last empty seat, which had a plate of warm food on it. I watched as Sade cooked more bacon and noticed she didn't look up or speak to me.

I glanced over at Beru, who had his head down and was shoveling food into his mouth like it was his last meal. He must not have been up much longer than me.

"You should eat before it gets cold." Sade finally acknowledged me.

I looked over at her, but she did not look my way. I'd take whatever she gave me. I just wanted our friendship back.

I waited patiently as Beru ate his breakfast. I wouldn't ask him until he finished. He had lost weight from being sick and needed to eat as much as he could. He glanced over at me, and I looked away. I didn't want to pressure him. I had to hold myself back.

I finished my breakfast and took it over to the wash bin. I kept my head down, but my eyes were on Beru. He was watching me as well. I walked over to sit by him.

"I don't want to rush you." I kept my eyes on the ground.

"It's time. Sade, Astor, and Iri, could you come over here?"

They came over and grabbed some stumps to sit on.

"I know who is tormenting this town and others." Beru paused and didn't look at any of us as his eyes filled with tears. "It's an ur'gel called Vinug. Have any of you heard of him before?"

Sade, Astor, and I shrugged, but Iri looked as if he recalled something about him.

"I thought he was in the prison." Iri straightened his back.

"He must have found the way out. He was one of the people that tormented me in prison. Then he freed me from the torture chamber and put me through something much worst."

"You don't have to talk about it if you don't want." I jumped in, seeing it was too much for him.

"I must for you to understand." His eyes pleaded with me to let him carry on.

"How do you know it's him?"

"The children. I should have known sooner. That's what he does. He takes their children to control them." He paused as if it was too much to go on.

"But I thought the prison only held Dag'draath and his soldiers." Sade entered into the conversation.

"When the walls went up, others were imprisoned. The people who lived in the valley before the prison was built. They had no notice to leave. They were able to live better than the prisoners, but only so they would have generations of soldiers for the ur'gel." He stood and paced.

I understood why he didn't want to stay and fight. He had been defeated over and over by Vinug. He wouldn't want to go up against him again, even with us.

"What happened to the children?" Iri finally broke the silence.

"Their parents sacrificed their lives so their children would go free." His back was to us. His voice quivered.

"We have to fight them, Beru." Sade stood and walked over to him, placing her hand on his shoulder, but he didn't turn around.

"There is no fighting him. He has an infinite number of ur'gel at his disposal. It would only mean more death."

"Sade is right. We have to help those people. We have to get their children back. We can't leave this to spread to other towns. Each child taken will only be a fighter for the ur'gel later as their army grows stronger, and we won't be able to win then." Iri stretched his back and pounded his fists together.

"We won't win against him." Beru turned back to us. "You don't understand how he works."

"He's a mesmerizer if I recall?" Iri added.

"Like no other." Beru hung his head.

I remained seated and rubbed my legs. They were sore from sleeping on a hard surface. I was used to luxury on the Islands.

I had to unite my team. Everyone was fighting against each other instead of fighting for our cause. Beru would usually take on anything, but he wasn't himself.

Iri and Beru talked about Vinug as Sade sat down beside me. She looked troubled and as if she wanted to talk to me. We sat still until she finally spoke. "I'm sorry about how I have been acting. Things are changing so quickly, and I've lost myself. My part in all of this." She put her face in her hands as if to hide.

"I'm sorry too. I need to listen more. To hear the people around me. I don't know everything." I half smiled. I didn't want to show how happy I was we were talking. She was so important to me. I needed her on my side always, and I wanted her happy.

"Let's just start fresh today. We need to get him ready to fight this Vinug."

"I agree with you on that. I think it may be an uphill battle, though." I watched as Iri appeared to be trying to convince him to stay and fight. Beru just kept shaking his head.

"There has to be something. I would want to stay and kick Vinug's ass for doing what Beru said he did." Sade looked over at the men as well.

There had to be part of him that wanted to do it. We just had to appeal to that side. I perked up with an idea. "I think I've got it. Something he won't be able to turn down."

"We'll trap him," I boasted to them. "We will always have the upper hand. He won't be able to refuse the bait." I might have been too enthusiastic with my idea.

"And I'm the bait?" Beru pointed to his chest with a look of disbelief at my plan.

"Sort of. And we will sweeten the pot with a dreamwalker. He won't be able to resist. We will remain in control at all times." I knew he would only go along with the plan if he knew I would do it without him. He wasn't one to sit on the sidelines, and he liked to look out for me.

"That's a crazy idea. I can't go along with it. You have no idea who you are fighting." Beru shook his head and crossed his arms as he pouted.

"Fine. You can sit it out, but I'm going ahead with it. He'll still want a dreamwalker." I stood my ground. I didn't know if Vinug would want me, but if he was working for Dag'draath, I'd be the perfect bait.

Beru stood a foot away from me and watched me intensely. His eyes didn't move from my face. I waited it out to see what he would do. I needed him to go with me.

"I'll do it," he finally stated. "If Vinug knows I am here, he will come. Or send his ur'gel after me."

Guilt came back full force as I knew, once again, I was pushing Beru to his breaking point. I knew he wasn't back to his full strength yet, but we needed him. Beru needed to do it.

"Let's break down this camp before anything happens. The giants kept watch all night and didn't see anyone approach our camp, but that could change at any time."

"On it." I saluted Sade with a smile. I was happy we had put our differences aside and were talking again.

I walked over to my makeshift bed and began to tear it down. Beru followed me and broke down his. Neither of us spoke as we worked. He was slower than me, so I took my time so we would be done at the same time.

I had packed everything carefully when I came across the stone Runa had given me. I wondered if she knew all we had been through since we last spoke. I placed the stone in my pocket in case I needed to talk with her if things went wrong.

"You sure about this plan?" He stood over his belongings and fiddled with some string.

"No, but are we ever? We must do what we think is right. It wouldn't be right to leave these people now. Not when they need us."

"That's one way of looking at it." He dropped the string to the ground and appeared to be looking for something.

"The barmaid said they sacrifice travelers. We'll take advantage of that. Then, when Vinug hears you are here, hopefully, he will make his appearance."

"And then what? What will you do once you have him?"

Beru looked like he needed more convincing for my plan to work. I thought about the different angles. How my plan could all go terribly wrong. But I didn't waver about what we would do if our plan worked. "We kill him."

"How?"

I wouldn't convince him this would work until it did. I picked up my bedding, took it over to the carriage, loaded it, and walked back to pick up my pack.

"So, you don't have a plan?" He followed me and loaded up his bed and pack.

"Just trust me." I regretted the words as soon as I spoke them. They would have been true before we dreamwalked but no longer. I held a huge secret from him. One I couldn't share just yet.

Sade came over and brought the plates and wash bowl to the carriage. She had already broken down her bed. "We ready to do this?" She looked at him and then back at me.

"Yes. Let's get this over with, so we can get back to passing through." I wiped my hands on my pants and gestured for Beru to walk with me. "We'll head down the road to the pub."

"I'll send a giant ahead. Iri, Astor, and I will follow behind you at a safe distance. We'll keep everyone within eyesight. If we lose sight of each other, this will go downhill fast." Sade nodded to both of us, and we agreed.

Beru and I took off on foot down the sidewalk. There were fewer people out than the day before, and we tried to look like we were sight-seeing. I pointed here and there, but Beru didn't entertain my plan. "We don't need to pretend. As soon as he knows I'm here, he will come." Beru kicked at the sand on the wood.

I'm sure, to passersby, he looked like he was pouting. I tried to keep the mood light as we slowed our pace. The giant was at his post by the pub, and when I glanced back, I saw the others had just turned onto the sidewalk.

"You're getting your appetite back. That's good." I tried to change the conversation. Who knew how long it would take for him to be noticed?

"The dizzy spells are lessening, but I can't get my head right." He looked tired.

"It will all come back. Just give it time." I put my hand on his arm, and he stopped walking and turned to me.

"Will it?" The dark circles under his eyes were more predominant in the sun.

I obviously had no way of knowing the future, but he needed kind words to get him through, and I owed him that. I couldn't put two words together in that moment, as I watched how vulnerable he was. "You've shown improvement each day, so it has to." I instinctively reached for his hand. "We're all here for you. Just lean on us."

He took my hand, glancing at our entwined fingers. "Things will be different now."

I nodded, unsure how, but I didn't want to question him. I'd wait for him to be more direct when he was ready. I pulled away from him and continued walking, missing his hand in mine immediately.

"Should we shop? Or keep walking?" I turned toward one of the grocers.

“Walk. The sun is nice.”

We continued but crossed the street. We stopped and looked at some of the items along the boardwalk but made sure not to enter any stores. I kept track of everyone else as we went along. The street was not awfully long so we would have to think of another way to get noticed soon.

“What did I miss while I was asleep? The dynamics seem to have changed.” He took a seat on a bench, and I sat down next to him.

“The ur’gel pushed through, as you’re aware. There were lots of raids. The only thing different was that we could retreat by ship.”

“I missed that?” He laughed. “How did you get Captain Rose to let Sade steer the ship?”

“She knew what damage they could do. We had to work within her schedule, but it worked out fine.” I reached into my pocket and pulled out a snack. It was an odd day. The weather was bright and brilliant, yet the looming gloom of our encounter with Vinug hung over our heads. Time seemed to stand still. We kept up simple chatter between silence.

Beru looked like he would nod off at any moment. I kept the conversation as light and engaging as I could. We talked to anyone who passed by, so people would talk about us. It was mid-day, and no one had appeared yet.

We hadn't discussed how long it would take. I had assumed it would be quick. I was running out of safe topics to talk about. We moved to the fountain in the middle of the main street. We watched as people threw coins in and made wishes. Such a childlike behavior. Another reminder as to why we were there.

"Here." I took two coins out of my pocket and gave one to Beru. "Make a wish."

"No. I have nothing to wish for, but you go ahead." He gently turned me toward the fountain.

I closed my eyes and didn't need to think long about what I wanted. I opened my eyes and tossed my coin in.

"Well, what did you wish for?"

"I can't tell. It won't come true." I smiled. I couldn't tell him my wish was about him. I continued to walk, and he followed me.

"How much longer do we have to be out here? I feel a sunburn coming on." Beru rubbed his forehead.

"We'll break for lunch." I made my way back to the boardwalk. I stopped to investigate the windows of a few stores and motioned for Beru to come with me into the soap store. "Might as well get things we need." I picked up some soap to smell and placed a few bars in my basket. The store was beginning to fill up compared to how few people were out shopping earlier.

“Get something for those giants,” Beru joked as he picked up a bar about the size of my head.

I carried on smelling most of the scents. I had never been in a store that carried so many before. I thought I would stock up while we had nothing better to do.

“Something is happening.” Beru leaned in and whispered in my ear.

I looked around us, and everyone had disappeared. Even the pay lady. There was no noise. I walked to the window, and there was no one on the street.

“I don’t see Sade or Iri anywhere. We better get outside.” I grabbed his hand, and we quickly left the store. We walked out into the middle of the road, which was empty. A lone basket rolled down it.

“Where did everyone go? I didn’t get any notice they had to leave. Did you?” Beru was as confused as I was.

“No, nothing. It’s as if they just vanished.” I walked a few paces away from him and searched for any sign of life.

“I don’t see them. This is not good. What if he has them and now we are in his trap?” Beru walked toward me. “Let’s keep close.”

I nodded and grabbed his arm. I wasn’t sure if he meant that close or not, but I was hanging on. Our plans had fallen through, and now my friends were at risk. We heard banging off in the distance. It resembled drums. It was getting louder, but the noise echoed, so we didn't know where it was coming from. However, it was coming toward us.

"They are here." Beru pulled me to his side, and I turned my head toward where he was looking.

A parade of ur'gel rounded the corner and walked toward us. They marched to the beat of the drum and chanted in their language. We didn't bother to run. They greatly outnumbered us. They surrounded us, and we were held captive in their circle.

They parted, and someone walked through. He was large and exotic looking, and I couldn't turn away from him. I was drawn in.

"Well, now. If it isn't Beru and the little dreamwalker." He smiled, and the corners of his lips almost met his eyes.

"It's Vinug," Beru whispered through gritted teeth.

"Thank you for freeing us." Vinug directed his comment to me as he jumped down from his horse. He walked over to us. "And my plaything has come back to me."

"I'd love to see what you'd have to say without the army behind you." Beru stood at ease as he waited for Vinug to respond to his threat.

"We want to talk." I stepped in front of Beru. "You need to leave this town alone and release the children." My eyes darted around as I tried to see where Sade, Astor, and Iri were.

"Are you looking for your friends?" Vinug walked over to me.

His eyes and smiled were mesmerizing and difficult to turn away from. I could feel my thoughts begin to change my opinion of him and I fought it. I wouldn't give in. I had to fight his charm and mindpower. "I don't know what you're talking about."

“I’m sure you don’t.” His smile pulled me in as I fought to keep a straight face. “Would you like to chat over a drink?”

He flirted with me to make Beru mad. He'd do anything to annoy Beru. He had us captive and possibly Iri, Astor, and Sade. My plan had turned upside down.

“No, neither of us are interested in having a drink with you,” Beru growled.

“You’ve changed. I can’t quite put my finger on it, but something is definitely different.” Vinug walked closer to us and eyed my hand wrapped around Beru’s arm. “No! It can’t be. You and the dreamwalker?” Vinug clapped his hands at the thought and then stroked his chin as he glanced between us.

“Let’s go somewhere alone. Just me and you.” Beru cracked his fingers as he inched closer to Vinug.

I stepped between them. Beru was going off-track, and I needed to bring him back. This wasn’t meant to be a revenge encounter. We had to focus on the village. Either Vinug came on board with our plan, or we had to kill him.

“Let’s go somewhere for that talk.” I focused on Vinug and hoped he would do the same and leave Beru alone.

“It didn’t take you long to get over your wife, did it?” Vinug smiled at Beru as he took a deep breath in.

“You can say whatever you want with all those ur’gel behind you. Let’s see what you say when you're alone with me.” Beru didn’t hold back.

They clearly had a history together but playing into that right now would not help us. We didn’t need to make Vinug mad. We had to convince him to work with us. Help us defeat Dag’draath. Somewhere deep inside him, he had to have hate for him. Before I said anything else, Beru stepped up and stood chest to chest with Vinug. Something caused me to pause. I saw something in Beru that had been hidden since he had slipped into that deep sleep. He was confident and ready to take on Vinug, even without our crew.

“I accept your challenge.” Vinug backed away from Beru and walked back to his army.

“What does this mean?” I grabbed Beru’s arm, afraid of what he may have just set himself up for.

“I guess we are going to fight.” Beru looked around as if he wanted to find something. Maybe he was looking for a weapon. Vinug had come armed, but we couldn’t exactly carry around swords and bows as we walked about town. We were prepared for hand combat if it came to that.

“It won’t be a fair fight.”

"I wouldn't expect it to be. I just need a stick. Something from hardwood." He looked toward the storefront. "One of those posts would work."

I looked over, and of course, it would work, but it was attached to the building. It would be hard to separate it with the army surrounding us. I swung my head around, looking for anything I could throw to him if it looked like he needed help. Besides throwing fruit, there was nothing to help. "He won't fight you with a weapon if you don't have one. It would make him look bad for fighting an unarmed man. He'll want to fight you fairly."

"He's not a fair man. But you may be right. We will have to wait and see. He's coming back now." Beru's back straightened as Vinug approached us.

"Are you ready, old man?" Vinug called to Beru as he unbuttoned his sleeves.

"More than you will ever know." Beru pulled off his shirt and flexed his muscles as he walked in a circle. He stretched out his arms and bent his neck back and forth.

"Good. We fight in one hour. By the town's fountain. Bring any weapons you have, as I will. The winner gets the town." Vinug nodded his head to Beru to confirm he understood.

"Got it." Beru shook out his hands as Vinug retreated to his army.

“Oh.” Vinug turned back. “And we fight to the death.” He smiled and continued.

“We don’t have to do this.” I pulled at Beru’s arm. He wasn’t ready for anything physical. He had just woken from a deep sleep and he hadn’t built up his appetite yet. He needed more time.

“I’ll do it. What do we have back at camp?”

“A sword or two. Mostly small knives. And anything Iri and Astor managed to get on their run yesterday.” I jogged to keep up with him.

“I’ll take it all.” He broke out in a run, and I followed. When we turned the corner to the camp, I felt relieved when I saw the others sitting by the fire. They looked agitated and just as happy to see us.

“Where were you? We looked everywhere,” Sade called angrily toward us.

“No time to talk. They found us and Beru is to fight him. We need all the weapons and whatever we can use as a weapon to take back.” I leaned over and placed my hands on my knees, out of breath.

“What? That’s mad. You can’t fight.” Iri stood up and joined us.

“Talking about it will just make us lose time. Gather everything up and follow us back.” Beru frantically searched the wagon for anything he could use.

We all searched through our personal items and dumped everything that could be used as a weapon in a pile. We stood back and took stock of what was available and frowned at the prospects.

“That’s not much.” I rubbed my face nervously.

“We couldn’t buy any weapons,” Iri added, obviously aware we were understocked for the fight.

“It will just be me fighting unless Vinug wins. Then he will come after each of you.” Beru looked around our circle.

“What does winning mean?”

“Death.” I didn't look up. Instead, I stared at the unimpressive pile of weapons we had gathered. My stomach felt weak. I’d brought this on Beru.

“You’re not serious. You agreed to those terms?” Sade grabbed Beru by the wrists and pulled him toward her.

“At least they were said,” he responded automatically. He pulled away from her and selected a few items from the pile.

“Let’s all grab the rest. We may need them to protect ourselves or give to Beru during the fight.” I loaded my pockets with the smaller items and then grabbed as much as I could with my arms.

We all walked back to the fountain together, loaded with our makeshift weapons. The ur'gel army had settled in and was working on a fighting ring. They had built a circular wall that came to Beru's chest. It would be difficult to get over the wall if we needed to intervene, which I supposed was the point.

"This is it." Iri dumped his items on the ground. "They are serious."

"He would be." I watched as Beru's eyes look over the ring. I turned my gaze to it as well and looked for any weaknesses or spots where we could help him when he needed it. It would be hard, but with the giants' help, we could get over the wall in a decent time.

Beru walked away from us. He paced in his own circle, swinging his arms up and down and then stretching.

I stayed back, careful not to break his concentration. He took off his shoes and jumped up and down. I watched his transformation from shy Beru back into being a warrior.

"You're not going to let him go through with this are you?" Sade asked.

"I can't stop him, and we can't exactly leave with this large army of ur'gel standing here." I waved my arm in their direction.

"Then you better get ready to fight. He's not ready to fight. Say whatever you need to say to him before it starts." Sade walked back to Iri and Astor.

I looked back at Beru. I couldn't tell him what I needed to before the fight. He needed his concentration to have any chance of winning.

A loud horn sounded, and the ur'gel took their places around the ring to watch the fight. Beru did one last stretch and then came my way.

"Are you sure . . ." I started to ask but he grabbed the back of my head and pulled me toward him. His soft lips touched mine and his tongue forced my lips open. We stood embraced for a fleeting time and then he pulled away and walked to the ring.

I stood shocked—speechless—at what had just happened.

"That was a long time coming." Sade came up from behind me.

My heart raced and I knew my cheeks and neck had turned scarlet red. I had not expected him to do that and I had little time to react and enjoy the moment.

Sade and I ran to the hoard and fought our way to the front. Beru and Vinug walked around each other as they waited for the second horn to sound the start of the fight.

"He's certainly come alive. He's looking more like the old Beru."

Sade was right. The fight seemed to invigorate him. I began to wonder if his family was his anchor or if fighting was. Even as he faced potential death, he remained calm.

The horn sounded, and I jumped. It was too soon. I wasn't ready.

Beru looked back at me and winked before he approached Vinug. His choice of weapon was a long sword, as was Vinug's. At least it would be an even fight.

Vinug swung first, and it was easy to tell he was a skilled fighter. He balanced the sword evenly and came through with a clean swing. He missed Beru, but the move seemed to be more for intimidation. He could have swung closer to him.

"Shit," Sade hissed under her breath.

They danced in a circle, careful not to expend their energy too fast. This would be a long fight. Each waited for the other to attack first.

Beru didn't wait long to begin. He swung his sword swiftly and with force, but he did not get close enough to hurt Vinug. Vinug took his turn. He swung just as hard as Beru and only missed him by a hair.

I let out a big breath when they each retreated for a short rest. It wasn't long before they were back at it again, with more force since they had gauged each other's strengths in the first round.

Vinug aimed for Beru's sword and knocked it out of his hands. Sade and I gasped, and I covered my mouth with my hand. Beru pulled out his small knife as Vinug attacked him with the sword. Blood from the sword wound slid down the small knife to his hand.

Beru jumped back to give himself space between them, but Vinug shortened the distance. He was relentless, apparently wanting it to be over. He was, perhaps, a little too overconfident because he rolled his ankle on the next strike. As he landed on the ground, the look on his face showed he knew what the mistake meant.

Beru leapt forward and kicked his sword away. He wasted little time sticking his knife in Vinug's neck. He stood and raised his arms over his head in victory. He walked around the ring, covered in blood and sweat, and showed no resemblance to the man who was sick and weak.

The ur'gel threw food and booed at him.

He brought his fists to his chest and growled at them. He turned to where Sade and I stood, and his attention was all on me. He walked in my direction confidently, his brown gaze penetrating my soul. My eyes were glued to his as I froze in place.

Beru still had it. He was indeed a warrior.

Beru burst through the ring and walked past us, making his way to the fountain. He dipped his hands in the water and washed the blood off his body. His demeanor was different. Overconfident, perhaps.

"What was that?" Sade asked.

"I don't know." I didn't want to turn my back on the army of ur'gel, but I also wanted to make some connection with Beru, especially after that kiss. I flipped back and forth between the two until it looked like the ur'gel were getting ready to disband.

"They are leaving." Iri stood in my view of Beru.

I tried not to look annoyed and stepped to the side as I watched him wash. It all happened so quickly, I was still on edge, waiting for the next terrible thing to arrive. I couldn't believe they would consider leaving us and giving the town back.

The ur'gel picked up Vinug's body from the ring. They wrapped him in cloth and loaded him into the wagon. They spoke in their language, so I couldn't tell what they were talking about, but they looked to be packing up to leave.

"I think they are. Shouldn't they stay and fight us?" I stood confused and shocked. Moments earlier, I was ready to tell Beru goodbye forever. Now I had to face him after that kiss.

"It would be disrespectful to Vinug's name to disobey the terms."

Instead of coming back to us, Beru began to walk down the street.

"Where is he going?" Sade lifted her hand in his direction and narrowed her eyes.

"The only thing that way is the camp," I offered. I didn't know if I should run after him or stay where I was.

"We should follow."

I nodded in agreement and reached over to Iri and pulled him along.

We made eye contact with the giants and Astor to follow us. We walked along the sidewalk, still expecting to be attacked at any point. I felt uneasy that Beru had gone on ahead of us without waiting.

We kept our eyes on him as he walked along the boardwalk. He picked up food from various vendors and would take a bite and then throw the item on the ground. He had never been a wasteful person. He was acting different. Maybe it was the high of potentially losing his life.

“I guess we should be happy he is awake.” Iri sounded confused as the words came out of his mouth.

I had a feeling deep in the pit of my stomach that I should somehow defend Beru. Almost against himself. But my head was telling me to be happy that he was not still in a deep sleep. We just needed to give him some time. He had to adjust to being a warrior again.

“He will have good days and bad days. Today was a good day. Let's just let him have his moment.” I tried to act like everything was normal, but I was worried about him. His reaction to winning was not what I expected.

We watched as he arrived at the campsite first. He kicked a few pots that were left on the ground and pushed a stump out of the way before finally settling down on a chair. He kicked up his feet and leaned back.

“And now we have a child in our midst.” Sade rolled her eyes.

“We have to give him some time to adjust. He’s been through a lot, and we have nothing to compare that to. We just have to be there for him.” I stood back, afraid to get closer to him, as he seemed even more like a stranger now.

"How are you doing?" Iri walked over to him and touched his shoulder.

Beru shrugged his hand off and I could tell that it offended Iri. They had become close friends over our travels together. Iri had stayed many nights alone with Beru when he was in his deep sleep.

"I'm fine." Beru stood up and walked over to find his pack. He pulled out some clean clothes and stripped down to change.

I looked away, embarrassed I had let my eyes linger a little too long. I watched as Sade's mouth scrunched up. She held back whatever wanted to fly out of it.

"We have to leave." Beru came barreling toward us with urgency.

"We will, once we know the children are coming back." Sade reminded him.

"No, we must leave now." Beru started to throw whatever was not already on the carriage onto it without a worry about breaking anything.

"Stop." Sade ran toward him with her hands up. Her personality would not be able to take this new Beru.

"If you had picked this up before, I wouldn't have to clean up." Beru stood his ground with her.

We all stood in our places in silence. We didn't know this Beru and weren't sure how far his tactics would go. I knew I could be the buffer, or at least I thought so. I wasn't sure if I wanted to test my theory.

Iri walked over and stepped between them before a fight broke out between the two of them. "I think you have had an exceptional day, so I'm going to give you a break. But I warn you—don't talk to Sade like that again." Iri's tone was firm but gentle.

The look in Beru's eyes changed. The anger receded, and he backed away without another word. He took a seat by the carriage and avoided any eye contact with anyone.

Iri walked over to me and pulled me aside. "Do we trust him? This isn't the guy I know."

I looked back at him, uncertain how I should answer. I felt like Iri did at that moment, but I couldn't turn my back on Beru while he was processing and dealing with everything that had happened. "Let's hear him out and proceed with caution."

Iri nodded, but I knew he was doing so reluctantly. He'd follow my command because he trusted me. I walked back to where my pack was and loaded it onto the carriage while Iri and Sade wandered off to talk alone.

"I know where we need to go." Beru came up behind me. "We have to leave soon."

"Where?" I finished what I was doing and then turned back to him.

His eyes were wider, and his facial expressions seemed more animated. "South. We need to go south." He grabbed my arms and shook me. He pulled back once he was done speaking and shook his head.

"What's south?" I questioned him.

"What?" He looked confused at my question.

I narrowed my eyes at his erratic behavior. "You want to go south."

Beru walked away from me and packed up the rest of our camp with a calmer and gentler demeanor. Sade and Iri watched us from a distance as if they were ready to pounce on him if he did anything inappropriate. I left Beru to finish up and walked over to them. I had seconds to determine if I was going to tell them about our conversation.

"Did he mention the kiss?" She wanted to know as soon as we were out of his hearing range.

"No." I had practically forgotten about the kiss given his new attitude.

"What did he say?" Iri put his hand on my back as if to protect me.

"That he knows we should go south," I told them quickly, while I had the nerve.

"What's south?"

“He wouldn’t say.” I turned my head just enough to see him.

Astor was with him, and they were laughing at something. He appeared to be his usual self again.

“What do we do?” Iri pulled me back into the conversation.

“He is the key. Maybe whatever we need is south.” My instincts told me to follow him. I could be completely wrong, but I decided to go with my gut.

“Let’s load up, then.” Iri walked past me before I could see his face.

“Is he mad?” My eyes followed Iri.

“He's never mad at you.” Sade offered a somber smile, then followed Iri.

We cleared camp and settled on who was riding and who would go in the carriage. Beru and I led, and the others followed. I wanted to get him alone to see if he knew why we should go south and where exactly we needed to go.

“How are you feeling? You’ve got everyone worried about you.” I used a warm tone and hoped he would not take offense.

“I’m good. I mean, as I can be.” Beru stared straight ahead.

“That was a tough fight back there.”

“He fell, and I got the better of him. If he hadn’t fallen, I wouldn’t be here.”

“You *might* not be.” I didn’t dare contradict him. He was right. He wasn't equipped to win a fight with a sword. I wanted him to keep talking, so I didn’t challenge him on anything he said.

“We need to pick up the pace.” He kicked his horse, and it sped up.

I tried my best to keep up with him. The carriage wouldn’t be able to go as fast, and I didn’t want to lose them. “We have to slow down,” I yelled at him, but he didn’t respond. “Wait,” I yelled even louder.

He slowed his horse, and I was able to ride alongside him again.

“What was that?” I grabbed onto his sleeve. I wanted him to look me in the eyes.

“You’re too slow. I have to get south.” He pointed ahead of us.

“The carriage can’t go that fast. We would have lost them.” My plan to talk slowly and warmly had quickly left. He was irrational, and I needed to call him out on it.

“They aren’t important.” He swung his arm back at them with an angry face.

"Excuse me?" Anger built inside me as I listened to him speak. Who was this person?

"I just meant they don't need to come. Just you and I will do." He kicked his horse and sped up again.

My anger got the best of me and I kicked my horse. Without a second thought, I jumped from my horse to his and knocked him to the ground. Both of our horses took off running in the other direction.

"Are you crazy?" Beru scrambled to his feet and readied himself for another attack.

"I was hoping another knock to the head would bring back your common sense." I walked a half circle around him, uncertain what I would do to him next.

"How are we going to get there now without horses?" He ran out to the trail to see if he could catch either horse, but they were long gone.

The carriage was coming down the trail, and I didn't think the others could have seen what had happened because they were too far back.

"Now what do we do?" Beru began to walk back to meet the carriage. "You're crazy. You know that?"

"I'm not the only crazy person here," I called to him.

It wasn't long till we were all together again. Beru told them what happened, and no one questioned him but looked to me for answers. I just confirmed he was right. I had jumped him. He needed to be taken down a notch. He was unhinged.

Beru and I jumped into the back of the carriage and sat as far away from each other as we could. How could we go from that kiss to this on the same day? We rode for miles and then Beru got up and sat next to me.

"I'm sorry. I don't know what's gotten into me. I haven't any patience lately." He held his head down and reminded me of a child who was forced to apologize.

"I don't know either. But I'll forgive it if you stop acting like this."

Beru nodded his head. "I know where we should go." He perked up.

"Where?" I hoped he would give more details this time. Maybe he remembered more.

"South. We need to go south." He acted like he had never told me that before.

"I know. You already told us. That's where we are heading." I pointed in the direction and wondered if he was trying to put me off to feel sorry for him.

"Right. My memory isn't what it used to be. I forget things. But I know we need to go south." Beru looked up at me, and his eyes were red and tearful.

If Beru couldn't remember things, what would be waiting for us in the south? Was it a trap?

"I don't know," Beru yelled abruptly before standing and walking away.

We had stopped for the day and were setting up our camp for the night when I decided to question Beru on his memory loss. I wanted to know how long it had been going on. I hadn't expected for him to get mad at my questioning.

I stayed seated by the fire to feed it the wood Iri had brought to me. Beru walked past the two giants and went into the woods. I debated with myself whether I should follow him, but I may drive him farther into the woods. He would come back when he was ready. I'd give him time to cool down.

"Mr. Moody just passed us." Sade dropped more wood in the pile. "What's his deal, anyway?"

"He told me he has memory loss. I think it's what angers him." I focused on my task, not wanting to get too involved in a conversation in case he returned.

"You'd think it would be the opposite. That he'd want to forget." She sat down next to me and began prepping food for supper.

She had a good point, but he was an alpha. "How is Iri doing? Between looking after Astor and Beru's attitude, I'm afraid he will quit on us."

"He's never leaving. He moans and groans about it." She smiled as if there was some sort of secret in what she said.

"So, is there a chance for anything to happen between you two?" I welcomed a change of topic.

"No. I'm fated to a wolf. He knows that." Her smile faded.

"You're engaged?" I sat back, confused.

"No, but if I want to mate, it must be with a wolf. It's their rule." She raised her eyebrows up and down and didn't offer any more information.

"I'm sorry. I didn't know that. What would happen if you didn't listen?" I pushed only because I was curious.

"It wouldn't be pretty. I've never known anyone who disobeyed."

She acted like it didn't bother her, but I knew it did. I had seen the connection she had with Iri, and that explained why she had never let it go any further. "Did you ever talk about it with Iri?" I couldn't help myself.

"There's nothing to talk about. What about you and Beru? That kiss he laid on you before the fight."

"You know as much as I do. I think he really thought he was going to die." I poured the chopped-up vegetables Sade had prepared into a pot full of water and began to boil them over the fire.

"Explains why he's kept you at arm's length since. I'm not sure I believe this memory thing. And I'm not on board with going south. I don't think any of us are." The skin under her eyes was dark and her eyes red.

I poked at the boiling pot and fought running away into the woods myself. I felt a loss of control and wondered if my instincts were right about following Beru.

"What are you thinking? For real. Not what you think I want to hear." Her tone was sweet and caring.

"I've been asking him about his memory loss. I keep wondering if it has anything to do with leaving the prison."

"He might not know how far back it started to happen. It sounds more plausible for it to have happened after your last dreamwalk."

I poked my stick in the pot, almost in a daze. I was so entranced I didn't hear Beru come back to the fire pit.

"Aria." He tried to get my attention.

"You're back." I turned my head to look at him and then returned to my duty of poking the pot.

"I just needed some time alone. I didn't want to blow up at you again." He put his hand on the ground behind me and leaned in. "Please have patience with me."

He didn't move after he whispered in my ear. I expected he was waiting for me to turn toward him. I shouldn't look at him, but the heat from his body called to me. I hesitatingly turned my head, and his face was mere inches from mine.

"You have to tell me more if you want me to understand." My eyes roamed from his eyes to his mouth. I half expected him to lean in and kiss me like before.

"Where did you go?" Sade spoke extra loudly to interrupt our moment.

Beru sat up straight, and I returned to poking the pot over the fire.

"I needed to clear my head. I'm sorry for how I have been speaking to you. I don't know why I'm acting like this." Beru's apology sounded sincere.

I looked up at Sade, but I couldn't get a good read on what she was thinking. Soon, Iri, Astor, and the two giants were back with more wood and straw for our beds.

“I think this should do it.” Iri dropped the hay over to where we had designated the sleeping area. And the two giants prepared the beds.

“Hmm . . . that smells good.” Astor sat down by the firepit. “When will it be ready?” He rubbed his hands together next to the fire.

“We just put it on.”

He made a grumpy face and then swiped a carrot that hadn’t made it into the pot.

“We scouted the area. No one has been through here for a while. I think we can rest easy tonight, but let’s not keep the fire going too late, just in case.” Iri drank from the flask that hung around his neck.

“Is there fresh water nearby?” Sade looked hopeful.

“A river not too far from here. We brought some back.” Iri nodded to a barrel.

Sade and Astor got up to fill their cups with water. I was thirsty but didn’t want to move. I could wait till later.

“How are things here at camp?” Iri cautiously spoke to me.

I’d let Beru answer and hope that the talking would help to mend their relationship. I wanted them to be close again. Beru needed Iri’s support. Iri knew more about his world before the prison than anyone did.

“I’m sorry about my attitude. Things are taking a toll on me, and I’m not handling it right.” Beru moved over toward Iri.

I watched from the corner of my eye to see what Iri would do next. He leaned over and grunted but didn’t speak. I knew Beru’s behavior toward Sade set Iri off. He would not tolerate anyone disrespecting her, and Beru had crossed that line.

“Just don’t let it happen again,” Iri finally responded.

“I won’t.” Beru shook his head, and we all fell into silence until Sade and Astor rejoined us.

“We’ve become boring.” Astor took his seat.

“I’m not boring.” Sade laughed.

“Let’s say we have a difference of opinion.” Astor smiled at her, and she pushed on his arm.

“Let’s say you’re sleeping on the most uncomfortable bed tonight.”

I laughed at the two of them carrying on. I envied their ability to push everything aside and have a little fun. I wished I could do that. I couldn’t help but feel off because of my worry for Beru.

I looked over at Iri and Beru. They were huddled together, deep in conversation. I couldn’t tell if it was good or bad, but they were both very serious. I tried my best to listen, but they were too quiet.

"Is it ready?" Sade asked.

I poked my stick inside the pot, and the vegetables were still hard. "No, not yet."

"I wonder what they are talking about."

"Will he tell you later?" I didn't know how close Iri and Sade were anymore, but I assumed they still had a very special friendship.

"Maybe. Hard to say." She took the stick from my hand and poked around the inside of the pot.

"I hope they can be friends again. Iri is good for him." I grabbed the bowls and laid them out on the ground.

"He has a big heart. I'm sure they will be fine. I'm more curious about Beru and you." Sade nudged my arm with a smile.

"He doesn't know who he is anymore, so I think that answers any question of a possible us." I let my disappointment show in my voice.

"Everyone." Beru stood up, and we looked at him, and then at each other, confused about what was going on.

Sade spoke first. "We're listening."

"I'm sorry about my behavior. I know you all have questions about me and my intentions, so I wanted to tell you all what I have been dealing with, besides what you already know. Please let me finish before you ask any questions. It has been many years since I've had to speak much to anyone." Beru rubbed the palms of his hands together and he looked deep in thought.

I looked over at Iri and thought this was his doing. He must have told Beru to come clean to everyone, so we would all feel good about our decision to follow him without knowing very much about why we were to go south.

"This goes back to Vinug. When I first arrived at the prison, I was tortured by him and his group or whatever you want to call them. It went on for a long time. Before I came to fight in the Great War, we were trained to suppress our memories. For these very reasons. I think the memories I suppressed are coming back to me now. It's the reason why I'm pushing for us to go south. I can't tell you any more than what I can remember, which is not much." Beru stopped to take a deep breath. "Any questions yet?"

"So, you have no idea what is south? How will we know how far south to go?" Astor flipped a rock back and forth in his hands.

I never really knew what Astor thought of Beru. They had gotten along alright, but they were never close. They rarely had conversations alone.

“I can’t answer that. I can only feel we are on the right road and I think I will know when we get there. I know that sounds ridiculous.” Beru looked over at me.

I didn’t have anything to add. He had already told me as much as he knew. I wanted him to know I supported him, but I wasn’t sure how to show it.

“Are you sure this isn’t a ploy to get us somewhere that could hurt us? Why can’t we follow through with Aria’s plan first?” Sade had no trouble asking questions.

“I can only explain it as a feeling. I think I would know if it was a trap and something to catch us. It feels like this is the answer we have been waiting for.” Beru chose his words carefully.

“I’m down with whatever the group decides. I’ve got nothing better to do.” Sade took the pot off the fire and began dishing out portions.

“I’m still going south with you,” I said.

Beru appeared relieved at my comment. I offered him a weak smile and handed out two bowls of soup with bread to the giants who were resting on the beds. I came back, and Astor had already claimed a bowl for himself, and Sade handed bowls to Beru and Iri.

“That’s quite the speech.” Sade sat beside me as Beru sat next to Iri in deep conversation again. “Believe him?”

"I guess. There's no one else alive he could be working with." I dipped my bread in my soup and ate it. I chewed too many times because I didn't want to speak anymore. I did believe him, but there was still some doubt.

"I'll go along for now." Sade slurped on her soup. "I'm getting another before the boys finish it up. You want more?"

"No, I've been munching away all day." I smiled and watched as she filled her bowl again.

I put my bowl down and rested my head on my arms. I let the sun beat down, and I closed my eyes to relax them. I was full, but my stomach felt empty. I braced myself for potentially having to shut down the trip at the first sign of it going wrong. I couldn't risk their lives for a feeling.

We started off early the next morning, as most of us didn't get a good night's sleep. Everyone was quiet as we moved along the trail. We had hoped to come across our horses but had no luck so far.

"Aria." Iri reached back and shook my shoulder. "We have company up ahead."

Four horses stampeded down the path in front of us. Their riders whipped their reins hard against the horses' shoulders, gaining speed.

"Let's stop here." I turned toward Sade and Beru, who were on horses behind us, and motioned to them that we were going to stop.

The carriage came to a stop, and I jumped down. Sade and Beru didn't have to ask why as they looked on ahead of us. Beru was the first to climb down from his horse, and he joined me as I walked out front.

"We outnumber them, at least," Beru offered as we stopped and waited for them to approach us.

"Unless they have others lagging behind," I replied, unable to feel optimistic.

They rode on and didn't seem to slow down. They were still far away, and it seemed to take them forever to reach us. That was enough time for my mind to worry.

"What's the plan?" Sade joined us with Iri.

Astor stayed on the carriage, and the two giants stood behind us. What a greeting committee. We didn't look threatening at all. "We greet them and see where they are headed. We should at least warn them about the town if they are friendly and going that way."

"Agreed." Beru bounced on the balls of his feet.

They slowed down as they got closer to us, which was a good sign. Each rider had bedding and pans, so they were traveling far. They stopped a fair distance away, and one of the men jumped down off his horse and approached us, while the others hung back.

"Greetings." He waved his hand as he spoke. "May I approach?" He stopped to wait for our response.

"Yes. Please come." I reached my hand out to him as he got near, and he shook it with a firm grip.

"Thank you. We were cautious when we first saw your party. I'm sure you understand." The man glanced at each one of us, pausing longer on the giants, clearly feeling uneasy.

"Yes. We are aware of what has been going on. How is this path? And the south?" This would be our first real indication as to what we were up against.

"It's not been untouched. I would turn around if I were you." He looked back at his people and nodded. They relaxed and dismounted their horses but remained together.

"Same thing ahead of you. May I ask why you are traveling?" I held my hand up to the giants and they dropped their swords to their sides. These were friendly people.

"I'm trying to get to my wife. She's with her mother. These are my sons and brother." He pointed to his party.

"Then we mustn't keep you." I smiled at the man and motioned for Iri to pull the carriage over so they could pass.

"Thank you. And good luck with your trip. Be careful." The man bowed and then ran back to his horse.

We moved the carriage, and I watched the men remount their horses and walk by us. Something inside told me their story wasn't entirely right, but whatever they were doing wouldn't hold us up any longer.

We carried on the path for some time, everyone lost in their own thoughts. Just as the silence became overwhelming, I suddenly felt dizzy and weak. I lay down from my seated position on the back of the carriage, my back bouncing against the wood as we traveled over the bumps and rocks.

"Are you all right?" Astor leaned over me.

"I'm fine. I just need to rest." I smiled at him to reassure him everything was okay. I didn't want him to alert the others.

I closed my eyes and rolled over onto my side, away from Astor and the two giants who walked on Astor's side of the carriage. Someone was calling me into a dream meeting, but I didn't know who. The presence was familiar, but they had not shown themselves to me yet. I just knew that it was not Runa. The feeling was unfamiliar.

I tried my best to focus as the carriage bounced up and down on the path, opening my mind to the one who was summoning me. Slowly, I sank deeper and deeper into a dream state until I was back in Mother Ofburg's house. Had she been the one who called me?

"Aria. Thank goodness you came to me." Mother Ofburg ran toward me with open arms. I embraced her, unsure what was going on and how she could have called me into a dream meeting.

"What's going on?" I was glad to have her back on my side, but worried at the same time.

“I need to ask a favor of you. I know the last few times we have been together, things were different. I was cold and mean.” Mother Ofburg grabbed my hands in hers. They were warm.

“It doesn’t matter. I handled things the wrong way.”

“No, listen to me. There’s something I need to tell you. It’s how I knew you were a dreamwalker. There was a prophecy about a dreamwalker from our village who would one day wake Dag’draath. The Healers council got together, and we vanquished all the known dreamwalker’s gifts. We thought we could stop Dag’draath from coming back.” Mother Ofburg’s hand began to shake in mine.

“But I could dreamwalk. It didn’t work on me.” I tried to make sense of what she was telling me.

“Only because your mother hid you. Your mother saved your gift. It was too late when we found out about you.” Mother Ofburg’s face grew pale, and she pulled away from me to sit on a chair. “It’s taken a lot of energy to reach you. I don’t have much time.”

I sat next to her and tried to process everything she had just said. “Is that why you took me in? It wasn’t my mother’s idea?”

“That’s not why I called on you. We need your help. Will you and your team come? We won’t survive if you don’t.” Mother Ofburg`s voice was quiet.

I began to feel the pull back to the present, but I held on. I tried to speak, but the words wouldn't come out of my mouth. I grabbed her hands again and tried to give her some of my energy so we could speak longer.

"What do you need our help with?" I tried to get her to answer, but she started to cry and wouldn't talk to me. I wasn't sure if she knew I was still with her anymore. It took everything I had to stay with her.

"Please come, Aria," she called out into the room, unaware I was right beside her, holding her hand.

"I'm coming, Mother Ofburg. I won't let you down. Can you hear me?" I yelled louder. I began to feel the bumps on the carriage ride, and I knew I didn't have much time left. "What is happening in the village?"

"They won't leave us alone," she cried out. "We can't fight them off."

"The ur'gel?" I yelled back at her, but she wasn't responsive to me.

"I hope you heard me, Aria." Mother Ofburg put her head in her hands and cried.

I hung on for as long as I could. I had to get back to the village to fight whoever was there. I prayed it wasn't Widow or anyone she was working with. They must have gone back for me.

I opened my eyes and was back on the carriage, but it had stopped. I rolled over onto my back to see Sade, Beru, Iri, and Astor standing over me. They were talking, but I couldn't hear what they were saying.

I tried to speak, but my mouth wouldn't move. I closed my eyes and opened them again, and they seemed to know that something was different. Slowly, my hearing came back, and I could hear them arguing about what happened.

Astor yelled at Iri for driving too fast and me bumping my head. I managed to sit up with their help. "It wasn't the drive. I was called to a dream meeting. It was Mother Ofburg. Something is happening in my village, and she wants us to come and help."

Everyone was quiet. I could tell I would need some encouragement for them to want to go with me. "I won't beg you all to come, but I must go. I can't leave them when they need me the most."

Sade leaned down and gave me a drink from her flask. "How is Mother Ofburg?"

"Not good. She was weak-minded. Crying uncontrollably. I've never seen her in such despair." I drank all the water in the flask and thought back to her face. I had never seen her cry before or ask for anything.

"Let's stop for lunch." Sade looked back at the boys. "It's early, but Aria needs some time to rest. We can decide after that what we will do. The village is east and not that far off where we were going."

Beru, Iri, and Astor nodded, and they jumped off the carriage.

"I'll get the fire going. Give her some time before she moves." Iri led the others into the woods for firewood.

"Mother Ofburg. Wow. How did she even reach you? She's not a dreamwalker." Sade sat down next to me.

"She must have had help, but all I saw was her. It wasn't very long. She couldn't hold the dream together, so I don't know much." I wanted to tell Sade about what Mother Ofburg had told me, but I didn't need another reason for them to dislike Mother Ofburg.

"What was it like seeing her again? After the last time." A soft smile fell on Sade's face.

Sade knew how important Mother Ofburg was to me, even if things fell apart in the end. "It felt like going home." I smiled. I hadn't realized how much I missed it. I had intended on never going back.

"I don't want to sound like a downer, but what if it wasn't her? What if it's Dag'draath's way to get you to come to him?" Sade interrupted my thoughts.

She had a point, but I would know if it wasn't the real Mother Ofburg. Her energy would be different. I was sure I would know. "I can't say for sure. I have to go with my gut. Even if it was Dag'draath calling me, I'd still go home if it meant saving my family."

"I'm not sure I want to go." Sade looked down. "I think you will have a hard time convincing Iri and Astor. They are already not wanting to go south."

"We were going to my village anyway. Before we decided to go south." I had to get Sade on my side. If she came, the boys would follow. Beru's opinion didn't matter at that point. I just had to convince Iri. Or even Astor. If Astor came, Iri would need to come.

"Are you able to get up now?" Sade stood and offered me her hand.

I reached up to grab it and grunted at the work it took to stand. I was in no shape to go to the village. It had been a while since I had dreamwalked, so getting back to myself would take longer. Another reason for them to not want to join me to help Mother Ofburg.

"I've got it. Thanks." I pulled away from her hand, walked to the end of the carriage, and jumped off. The ground seemed closer than I thought, and I fell over.

"You're not all right Aria." Sade helped me to my feet.

"I'm not, but I will be. I just need to sit down by the fire and rest a little. Food will help." I convinced Sade to take me over to where they were starting a fire.

"Sit here." Beru motioned to Sade to drop me on a bed of hay.

She took me over and helped me get on the ground without falling on my face. Beru handed me a drink and sat down next to me. "I'll go with you."

Everyone stopped what they were doing to look at us. They seemed irritated Beru had spoken up first when they were still on the fence.

"I'll go too." Sade was next.

"Me too," Iri called out.

"Okay, I'll go." Astor let out a massive sigh and then filled his mouth with food.

I smiled at my friends and their loyalty to me. We could help Mother Ofburg and then get back on the road to go south.

We changed directions as soon as we packed up. My village wasn't too far out of the way. I lay down on the back of the carriage in case Mother Ofburg tried to contact me again. It would be easier than if I was on one of the horses.

As I lay on my back, I stared up at the sky. The bright sun and cloudless sky were contradictory to the inner turmoil I held inside. My fear for my family kept me moving east. Even after the way I left things with my brothers, I'd still give my life to keep them safe. Ironically, the war started with that same devotion I had for them. One they all threw away so easily.

The two giants chose to walk. Both men had stayed silent our entire trip, keeping us safe for such small coin. I knew nothing of either of them. Did they have families? Why did they agree to take on this quest with us, knowing their lives were in constant danger?

Astor sat with Iri as he drove the carriage, so I had the back to myself. I packed some hay down, so each bump and hole on the path didn't send my body flying as much into the air.

I closed my eyes and tried to remember what Mother Ofburg had told me and if there was anything I had missed. I replayed the dreamwalk over and over. The desperation in her voice brought tears to my eyes. There was no way it was a trap. Someone was tormenting her, perhaps to get to me.

I opened my eyes again and took in a few deep breaths to calm myself. There was nothing I could do until we got there. I had to stop reliving that moment, but every time I closed my eyes, I saw her face and the tears as they rolled down her cheeks.

I sat up, and my eyes found Beru and Sade, who rode behind the carriage, and both of their eyes were on me. I lay back down on my side, not wanting to talk.

My thoughts switched to my family. I hoped they were safe and whatever had Mother Ofburg so scared hadn't hurt any of them. My thoughts drifted to my niece and how much I had missed of her growing up already. I'd finally get to hold her in my arms.

I wiped the tears off my face, which I hadn't noticed falling. I had to prepare myself to see my family as well. To hear them chastise me again—if they even opened the door when I arrived.

I heard someone from the front of the carriage stir. They made their way back to me. It was easy to guess who, just by their size. “I’m here for you, Aria.” Iri placed his hand on my shoulder.

I wiped the rest of my tears and sat up. “Are you sure you want Astor driving this thing?” I partially joked with him.

“The horses know what they are doing.” He offered me a smile and passed me an apple. “Food always makes it better.”

I grabbed his offering and took a bite. The pie lady was right. They were the best apples ever. We both ate our apples quietly, and I glanced back at Beru and Sade, who looked to be having a friendly conversation. They both smiled and appeared to be joking.

“It’s nice to see things look like they are getting back to normal.” Iri watched them as well.

“It is. It didn’t seem like it would be for a while.” I steadied myself and sat up on one of the benches opposite Iri.

“No, it did not.” Iri half smiled.

Iri had proven to be a wonderful friend to me. He reminded me of my father, and I knew I could tell him anything, and he would give me the best advice. It was a pity he never had any of his own children. He would have made a wonderful father. But I don't think he would have ended up being the great warrior he became.

"Thank you for following me blindly wherever I seem to want to go. And I know I ask you to follow blindly." I took another bite of my apple as Iri shoved the last piece of his in his mouth.

"We believe in your cause." Iri reached over and patted my knee. "You're not asking too much from us. We have always fought evil. Now we fight together."

I put my hand over his and smiled. He made me feel at ease and deserving of their affections. "Thank you. There's no other team I would want to be with."

"*Whoa*!" Astor called as he pulled back hard on the reins to stop the horses. I held onto the side of the carriage, so I wouldn't fall back onto the ground.

"What is it?" Iri jumped down from the back of the carriage and helped me get down. Beru and Sade jumped off their horses and we all rushed up front with Astor.

"They barricaded the road." Astor pointed to the thick mound of trees in our path.

It was the only road to the village, and the trees were too dense to take the carriage through another way. It would take at least two days to pull the large trees down with our horses.

"We have to leave the carriage here." Beru said what I didn't want to.

We'd have four horses to travel with. Not enough for everyone to go. We would have to choose who was more valuable.

"I can't leave Astor." Iri said.

"Not even with the giants?"

"They'd have no way of getting away fast."

"We could leave them a horse." Beru was quick to find a solution.

Iri walked away from us and pulled Astor aside. He placed his arm around his shoulders, and they turned their backs to us.

"Do you think he will leave him?" I looked toward the one who knew him best: Sade.

"I don't know. It would be hard for him if he did and something happened to Astor." She watched as intensely as I did.

They finally broke up and walked back to us.

Iri took a few moments to tell us his decision. "Astor will ride with me on a horse. Then Beru, Sade, and you will each have a horse. The giants will stay behind with the carriage. This isn't their fight. We will do our best to hide it, so they are not spotted." Iri's decision was final.

There was no chance of changing his mind, and no one tried.

"Let's do this, then." Sade walked over to the carriage and jumped on the back to rummage through all the items.

I jumped on to help as well. We didn't have much in the way of weapons—we hadn't been able to arm ourselves in the last town, and what weapons we had before were long lost from Beru's battle. The ones we had left were for close combat.

"I hope they have something there we can use to fight." Sade stretched, sighing.

"I still have some things hidden in my family's barn. We could stop there first." I dug straight to the floor to make sure we didn't leave behind anything useful.

"Let's do that. We'll be better off fighting with rocks than anything here." Sade nodded and got off the carriage. "Need help?"

"I got it. I'm feeling better. I'll be good once we get there." I jumped down and felt all my muscles tense as I hit the ground.

We packed what we could and loaded up the horses. Iri, Astor, and Sade led while Beru and I hung behind them. We left the giants to hide the carriage and told them we would be back as soon as we could.

We headed off into the peaceful forest. I inhaled the sweet smell of the pine trees and relaxed with the soft sounds of the horse's hoofs as they walked through the grass. Sade and Iri bantered quietly in front of us.

“How was your ride with Sade?” I looked over at Beru, who seemed to be enjoying the walk in the woods as well.

“Good. I hope. I have some things to prove to her, which will take time.” He smiled at me and kept whatever pace I lead.

“I’m glad.” He seemed like the old Beru. More reserved and easy going.

“The bigger question is where do you and I stand now?” Beru rode his horse closer to mine and lowered his voice so only I could hear him.

“What do you mean?” I fully knew what he meant. At least, I thought I knew. We hadn’t spoken about our impromptu kiss and the way Beru had been acting. It was like he wanted to forget it happened.

“I think there has been this big question as to where our relationship would go. I’d like to think that it was going in the direction we both wanted before we arrived at the Island.” Beru’s gaze was intense yet friendly. This was the first time in a while he appeared to be back to himself.

"I think that's something that may come with time." My cheeks warmed. We had to wait till this was all over—till we had nothing to fight but falling in love. I knew I wanted him, but I had to tell him I controlled where we went in the dreamwalk. That I tried to break him so he would remember.

"So, I haven't lost my chance?" He smiled but kept his head down.

"No." I wasn't sure if there was an inch of my skin that wasn't red.

We rode on for a while with neither of us talking. It was awkward yet exciting. It was our first real talk about us, and it felt good to have it said out loud and not to wonder if he liked me or not.

"You two okay back there?" Sade looked back at us.

"Just enjoying the ride before whatever we have to face," I called to her.

Sade seemed to accept my reply, and she turned back to her conversation with Iri and Astor.

Beru eased his horse out a little to give me more space. If we weren't heading into battle, it would have been the most romantic walk I had ever been on. I glanced over at Beru, and he was watching me. I caught his eyes as they searched my body. My cheeks flushed even brighter as I wondered what he was thinking about.

"You feel up for fighting?" Beru changed the subject.

"Yes. I used a lot of what you taught me in the raids. You would have been proud." On our long trip, Beru and I had practiced fighting on our breaks. I was once even able to flip him on his back, even though he claimed he let me.

He had taught me to fight smarter.

"I'm glad. You were getting stronger. Your reflexes quicker." Beru nodded his head as he remembered.

"I'll be harder to beat next time." I teased him but then felt angry I was keeping a huge secret from him and acting like we were going to move on like a couple. When he found out, he'd leave me. I had to keep it a secret until the prison was closed again. Then we could sit down and talk about it. Maybe, with more time away from the dreamwalk, he could forgive me.

"I'm not sure about that." He laughed out loud. "But I hope you do well today. And if not, I'll always be close." His voice turned serious.

"Stand back." Sade and Iri had stopped up ahead of us.

We pulled on our horses' reins to stop, and we all listened to the woods. There was movement. It was not close, but we were coming up on someone or something. Sade waved us to move over closer to them.

"How far are we away from the village?"

"Not far at all . . ." I stopped talking as another rush in the brush alerted us. It was closer. Whoever or whatever it was, knew we were there, and it sounded like it was making its way back to the village. We wouldn't have surprise on our side anymore.

"We'd better make a move on it before they get back." Iri pulled on his reins and took off down the path. We all followed, riding as fast as we could. We'd have to be ready for whatever we saw as soon as we arrived in the village.

Sade and I left the boys, creeping toward the village to gather as much information about what was going on as we could. We snuck up to some thick brush and lay down to we wait to hear or see anything unusual. It didn't take long to find out Widow had surrounded the village with her spiders.

She floated around as if she were queen. She held all the village people in a dome spun from her web. Her spiders kept bringing people to it.

"Wow." Sade murmured. "That's impressive."

"Not for us." I grimaced at her odd comment.

"Sorry. I've just never seen anything like it." She marveled at its construction.

"I want to get closer. I need to see if any of my family have been captured. Can you watch me?"

"Where do you plan to go?" Sade looked surprised I would want to go out there.

"That barn." I pointed to the closest hiding spot that wouldn't cause any concern.

She gave me a nod and I ducked out from behind the brush and made my way to the barn. I dashed forward and looked back at Sade, who gave me another nod. No one had seen me.

I crouched down and moved closer to the dome. I hid behind a bushel of hay. My eyes scanned the dome or what I could see of it for any of my brothers or my parents. I saw neighbors who lived close to my parents' farm, so I knew she likely had them captured, maybe somewhere more secure because she knew I would come for them.

My head jerked back as I caught a glimpse of Vinsha in the dome. She stood alone, and I wondered where her baby was. I couldn't risk trying to catch her attention in case she drew attention to me.

I sat back against the barn to process what I had seen. I speculated where they were keeping Mother Ofburg. In my dreamwalk, she was still in her house. I got back into my position to see if I could see her in the dome but had no luck. Widow had spun her webs so there were few spaces for anyone to see in or out.

I tried to find Vinsha again, but it was useless. They were filling up the dome quickly, and it was getting harder to see people inside as she built up the walls. I crawled back to the brush where Sade was hiding out.

"What did you see?" She wanted to know as soon as I was by her side again.

"She has Vinsha. And some farmers that live by my parents." I looked through the brush to get a better view of the whole operation.

"What about the baby?"

"She was alone." I turned back to Sade. "She must have my family. She has Mother Ofburg. She wants me. I can put a stop to all of this."

"Don't fall for her trap. She's strategic. We have to think this out instead of running out there and attacking anyone who dares stop us." Sade put her hand on my shoulder and squeezed it.

She was right. Widow had time to put this together. She had a brilliant mind, and we had to think like she would. There would be a reason behind everything she did, and it was likely a trap.

"Let's head back to the boys." I started to get up, but Sade pushed me back down and put her hand over my mouth.

Then I heard the footsteps on the other side of the brush. I closed my eyes like I had when I was a kid and we were playing hide and seek. As if the finder could not see me. The footsteps stopped, and we held our poses. Soon, they moved on. We waited for a while and then

Sade lifted her head a little to see if anything was still close.

"We're good. Let's get back before we can't. I don't want them charging out here to save us."

I went first. I made my way farther back to some thick brush and waited for Sade to join me. Once she met me, we could afford to be a little louder as we made our way back to the boys.

We came across the empty barn where we'd agreed to meet. The horses were left deeper in the woods to lessen any noises.

"Finally." Beru grabbed me, pulling me into his arms.

He caught me off-guard, but I let myself melt into his embrace. I didn't know if it would be our last. "Sorry," he mouthed to me as I pulled back.

"We scouted as much as we could. They have a dome, and they are holding people there." I walked over to the desk and drew a floor plan of what I had seen in the dust. "Over here."

"She's been here for a while, then?" Iri's eyes were wide.

"A few days at most. They are still gathering people. If they knew she was here, they would have run."

"And there are lots of them. We would be crazy to go in there with just us." Sade leaned over and watched what I was doing.

"Can we make it to your farm? Get weapons?" Iri reiterated the former plan.

"They have my sister-in-law. They will have already been there and ripped every inch of it apart."

"No sight of Gavin?" Beru's voice sounded worried as he looked at me from his corner of the desk.

I shook my head and returned to my dust drawing. I fought off tears at the thought of Gavin having to defend himself against Widow and her army of spiders. He wouldn't have been able to get away fast enough to save himself.

"We'll find him." Sade pulled my head next to hers. "I promise."

I nodded, wiping away the tears I had let fall. I needed to find my family, and the best way I knew how was to get this map down before I forgot where her reinforcements were.

"We should bring help in to attack them." Iri paced around the small barn.

"Who?" Sade lifted her head up to him,

"The D'ahvol. They would *crush* these spiders." Iri slammed his hands together to emphasize the word crush.

“You’re forgetting they hate everyone. Especially me.” I looked up from my work at Iri, surprised he had forgotten.

“It was a thought.” Iri shrugged and continued to pace around.

I looked at my map and closed my eyes to visually remember what I had just seen. Where the dome was, where the guards stood, and what buildings they had taken over. I compared my visual to the map and nodded when I had accounted for everything. “I think that’s it.”

I stepped back, and Sade took my place, looking at each point.

“There was another guard here.” She marked an X on the spot and at the back of the dome she marked another X.

“There’s no way we could get in there without being seen,” I mumbled, more to myself than to the others.

“What about magic?” Astor spoke for the first time. He had been holding back since we left the ship. He was not a fan of fighting and wasn’t any good at it. It was better for us to have him held back so we wouldn’t have to worry about him.

“I don’t know.” I rubbed my chin. I couldn’t count on Astor’s ability to do magic when it could risk our lives, but I wouldn’t tell him that. It would crush him.

"I could put something together easily." Astor practically knocked Sade over in his excitement.

"Maybe, but we should think of other options too." I looked at Sade, who stood out of Astor's view and mouthed, "No."

I needed it to be quiet, so I could think, but it would be a risk to walk outside. I tried to get inside my head, to drown out Astor who proclaimed he would save us all. Sade stood there arguing with him. I looked around for Beru. He stood off in the corner and kept to himself. He looked deep in thought. Iri still paced the room, blocking out Astor and Sade as well. I don't even know why Sade entertained Astor. He knew every string to pull with her and enjoyed it.

"She needs me, Sade." Astor roasted Sade with a smile.

Sade gave him the worst look she had and then walked over to Iri, who hid his smirk. I pushed their silliness aside as I remembered another post by the water. I had seen at least three spiders spinning webs from there. It would be difficult making our way in from any direction.

"Where is the most likely place for her to hold your family or people she thinks you would come back for?" Sade focused her attention on me.

"She could have another dome somewhere else. The web is sticky, so it would be hard to get through."

"We could set it on fire," Astor piped in.

"Then everyone would die." Sade rolled her eyes.

I wasn't sure how much longer I could listen to them while I tried to think of something—anything we could do without sacrificing ourselves. I stood back and looked at the map from another angle. There had to be a way to get in without being seen. She couldn't have eyes everywhere.

I walked around the table and looked through every vantage point. Nothing came to me. I went through it all again. She couldn't have everything blocked off. There had to be a way in without her knowing.

"What if I went in and acted like I was just a farmer? I could make it to the dome and talk to people and then use magic to get myself out," Astor suggested.

"I'm tempted to let him," Sade whispered in my ear.

I smiled at her. "That's a good plan. I'll keep that in mind." I went back to my drawing, and suddenly, an idea came to my mind. I fleshed it out as Sade and Astor bickered in the background.

"I got it." I tried not to scream. "I know how we can get in there without getting caught in any traps." I beamed at my idea and felt foolish I hadn't thought of it before.

“Well?” Sade was clearly annoyed I hadn’t just come out with the plan.

“I’ll dreamwalk but as a projection. I won’t use my body.” I smiled and waited for them to catch up.

“You can do that?” Beru walked forward into the room from his corner.

“I can still be there and not be seen.” I lifted my hands up and waited for them to ask the inevitable question.

“Can we come too?” Sade seemed interested.

“No. I’d go alone. I’d need all the energy I could muster for this.” I leaned over my map to study it.

“I’m with you on this, but we need more details.” Beru placed his hand on my back, and I could feel its warmth through my clothes.

“You all need to be in a safer place. Somewhere far away. Then I will dreamwalk from there but only as a projection of myself, so I can’t be harmed if things go wrong.” Beru was the first to understand and agree with what I was saying. Iri and Astor didn’t say much, and Sade was likely mad she wasn’t going with me.

“What will you do once you’re in?” Sade crossed her arms, unhappy with the plan.

“I’ll go to Widow and see what she wants. Try to get information on Dag'draath to see if he is out or not. She wanted me to work with them. I could pretend that I still am." I watched as Iri came around to my idea next.

"So, she couldn't hurt you? In any way?"

"No. It would only be a projection of my image, and I'd use less energy, so I could stay longer if I had to convince her we wanted to work together."

"Could we wake you out of the dreamwalk if we had to?"

"Yes. It would be safe." I had to convince them it was the right plan, even if it meant I had to lie. I didn't have enough experience with projection to have a definite answer for them.

I took one more glance at my map. "Let's head out."

We relied on Sade to find us a safe spot where I could dreamwalk. She knew every crevice in the woods no else had ever been. We walked away from the village but kept on guard because the spiders were likely to patrol the woods so they could capture anyone they found.

"It's not much further now," Sade called over her shoulder as we walked single file in the woods behind her.

The brush was thick, and it was difficult to be silent as we walked through. I broke off a branch from a tree to help hold the other branches back as much as I could. We needed to be mindful of how much noise we made.

"It's over here!" Sade called.

The brush was too thick to see her, so I followed the path her body had made through the bushes. I pushed through until there was a little opening and there was the mouth to a cave. I helped the boys out of the brush with my stick and then we all went into the cave.

"This will do." I smiled once inside. We could see over the valley from inside the cave and see anyone coming way before they reached us.

"I have some things hidden in the back. Not enough for everyone, but comfortable enough for you to dreamwalk," Sade explained. "Iri." She glanced over her shoulder. "Can you help me?"

"Of course," Iri answered gruffly as he walked deeper into the cave with Sade.

"Hard to picture Sade living alone." Beru put his pack down on the ground.

"Not really. It took a lot of work breaking her in."

"I'll be back. I'm going to erase as many of our footprints as I can." Beru touched my arm before he left, and for a moment, I thought he would kiss me again.

"I can do a spell." Astor's voice came from behind me.

I almost jumped a foot in the air. "I know it's been a while since you have done any magic, but let's just keep it for when we need it."

"I have been practicing. Those walks I have been taking. I'm just here and willing to do my part." Astor looked defeated, and I immediately regretted my tone with him.

"I know. You're an important part of this team, but you know how some of your spells have turned out. Not the way you wanted them to." I hated being the bad guy, but I had to come clean with him. He had to know how important this was. We couldn't chance it on a failed spell.

"In other words, when we have no absolute chance, then Astor can do his magic?" Astor painted a smile on his face.

I leaned in and hugged him, whispering in his ear, "I'm sorry."

"It is what it is, I guess." Astor shrugged as Beru came back into the cave. "Just making a move on your girl." Astor laughed as Beru stared at the two of us embracing.

"All set?" I asked, pushing away from Astor.

"Yeah, I cleared our tracks from the point of the road." Beru entered the cave.

Sade and Iri came back with several barrels of items. Beru and Astor helped them unload.

"There's makings for a bed here somewhere." Sade poked around and opened the barrel.

"It's here." Beru pulled out the bedding. "Where would you like it?"

"Over here should be fine." I picked the driest spot close to the opening of the cave.

Beru made up my bed as the others looked through all the items Sade had hoarded in the cave. Once my bed was made, I lay down and got comfortable. I didn't want to wait any longer. I knew what the layout was, and I couldn't be sure it wouldn't change if we didn't move fast.

"I'm ready. I won't be gone long. I'll come back at any threat of danger. You all know how it is, but please be quiet to not disturb my body. I don't want them to know I'm projecting. This may be the one chance that we have." I looked at each of them for a nod of acknowledgment.

"I'll keep them in check." Sade smiled at me as she placed a pillow under my head.

I closed my eyes and felt nervous. Dreamwalking felt normal to me now. I only stayed away from it as it had done harm to my body. I had aches and pains I didn't have from before.

I let myself drift off. I'd start my walk on the path and enter from the barn. I wasn't sure where to go to find Widow, but I knew she would come to me. I ran down the path, unafraid of being discovered. If I were found, that would save me some time. Then, I realized how far back on the path I'd started. I groaned. It would take me longer than I'd hoped to get to the village on foot.

I picked up my speed as a drop of rain fell on my face. "Great." I didn't stop running, even as I ran out of breath. I kept going until I was in familiar territory. At the end of the village, I took to the woods. Back to where Sade and I were hiding. I ran to the back of the barn and surveyed the area. The dome was completely covered, and I was unable to see inside but could hear the people who were being held captive crying and yelling.

The quickest way to Widow would be to show myself in the open. I had nothing to lose, so I ran out into the village and tried to make my way to the dome. I was stopped before then, which was what I wanted.

The spiders surrounded me. I couldn't see through the thick of all their legs. A horn sounded and they all parted. A path appeared as they stood on each side of it and Widow walked toward me. "Aria, finally." She was in front of me in no time. I barely had time to blink. "Come. We must dine." She snapped her fingers, and the spiders left.

"I heard you were here, so I came." I smiled and pretended we were still on reasonable grounds, as she seemed to believe.

"I thought you might. Sorry about the village." She waved her hand around. "I know you lived here at one time."

“I hated it.” I smiled. “I wouldn’t have come if you weren’t here.”

“Oh? Don’t you have family or other here?” Widow raised an eyebrow as she looked down on me.

“I do, but they threw me out a while ago. You can’t please everyone.” I followed her into a large tent. Inside, there was a large bed fit for Widow and a table—which was set up for supper.

“Please sit.” She gestured to the smaller seat, and she removed her coat and sat in the larger seat. “I’ve been curious as to your adventure on the Islands.”

“It didn’t have the answers that we were looking for.” I smiled as I dipped my fork in my food.

“Yes, I heard you were in search of the key?” Widow leaned in.

I wasn’t sure how much she knew about the key and if she knew it was Beru, but I’d play along to see if she would tell me more. “Yes, I was. But it turned out to be nothing more than a legend.” I tried my best to show disappointment.

“I was surprised that you hadn’t freed poor Dag'draath yet.” Widow started eating the food on her plate.

I looked around the room for any clues as to why she would be there. She apparently thought we were both on the same side, so why set up camp in my village?

“You like it?” She pointed her fork in the air and waved it around. “I had it ordered from the slave children.”

I coughed on my food. “Slave children?”

“Oh yes, a great new addition. I can get you one too if you like.”

“No, I’m good.” I smiled and focused on cutting up my meat. Widow rambled on about decorations, and I tried my best to look interested in what she was talking about.

“So, enough of this talk. Let’s discuss Dag'draath and how we are going to free him. How did you do it with that other one?” She waved her fork in the air again. “With that handsome piece of man meat.” She looked like she wanted to eat him.

“He was a test, of course. To see how I could get someone out. It was by mistake, mostly. I’ve not been able to replicate it since.” I lowered my lashes. I was a fair liar, but Widow was smart. I mustn’t be too arrogant in my approach with her. She could very well outwit me in my own game.

“I see. Will you make another attempt? Dag'draath is growing impatient. It’s hard to witness.” Widow shook her head, almost as if she was implying they were a thing.

"You have been in the prison?" I perked up at the thought. How could she have gone without dreamwalking?

"No, we communicate telepathically. I'm much more powerful than a dreamwalker. Oh, sorry. I didn't mean anything by it." She shoved a giant sausage in her mouth and moaned.

"I'm not offended. I know you have great power. That's why teaming up with you makes sense." I smiled and fought back a look of disgust. I needed to know what she knew without her catching on that I was fishing for information.

"Of course, you're not. Now, Dag'draath has felt you poking around the prison." Widow pointed her fork at me as she narrowed one eyelid. "But he's not felt you in a while."

"I've been away on the Island, as you know. They have a ban on dreamwalkers there. It was impossible to get away from. Another reason we left." I rolled my eyes to show my annoyance with their rules.

"I see. And have you dreamwalked since you left the Island?"

I filled my mouth with food and shook my head. I watched as Widow grew curious at my activities. A little too interested. I had to turn this conversation around. I needed to find out why she was in my village and what she was doing with everyone. And where was Mother Ofburg? Had she made her dreamwalk to the prison?

All those questions raced through my mind. I needed answers, but I couldn't pelt her with too many things at once. "That's quite an impressive dome you built. A great way to hold people."

"Yes, a prison." Widow smiled, clearly impressed with herself.

I took a big gulp of water and hoped she would tell me more if I talked less. Instead, she waved to her servant for another plate of food. Once it arrived, she told everyone to leave the tent. "There, now we can talk without additional ears. I'm very interested in your visits to the prison." Widow ate more from her plate but kept an eye on me.

"It's not a happy place. I'm sure you have heard that. It's dark and grim." I hoped her line of questions would reveal her knowledge of the prison.

"And can you dreamwalk there at any time?" She changed her tone, so it was different than the rest of her questioning.

I knew it was a baited question, and I had little time to think about how I was going to answer her. "It doesn't work like that." I wiped my mouth with a napkin.

“Go on. Do tell.” She sat back and brought her wine glass to her lips, her eyes steady on me.

“I was connected to Beru. I didn’t have a choice when I dreamwalked then.”

“And now? You’ve been back since you freed him. How?” Her tone grew darker.

“I’m connected to something there. But I’m not sure what.”

“Or who,” Widow quickly added. “Would you indulge me?”

I agreed, for if I denied her, our talk would be over, and I wouldn’t get any answers.

Widow got up and pointed to her bed. “Will you try to dreamwalk to the prison now?”

“I’m much too weak.” I blotted my lips again. Widow remained standing, and her gaze almost looked through me.

“Then will you do something else to show your allegiance to me and Dag'draath?” Widow walked around the table to stand behind me. She leaned in and whispered, “Kill Mother Ofburg.”

Before I even had time to answer Widow's crazy question, she rang a bell that sat on the table. As the ringing echoed through her tent, I heard muffled sounds coming from a little room off to the side that was covered with a blanket. Two human servants brought out a chair with a person tied to it. As they entered the room, the chair was pointed backward. Once they got closer, they turned it around, and Mother Ofburg sat on it, her mouth taped shut.

"We were just speaking about you." Widow patted the side of the table, and the two humans placed Mother Ofburg in that spot.

Her eyes widened when she saw me, but I turned away from her. I didn't want Widow to know I loved her. She would use it against me, so I needed her to believe she meant nothing. "Kill her. I don't care. I'm sure you have heard she threw me out of her house. More than once."

Widow broke out into evil laughter, and one of her hands came down hard on the table as she slapped it. “I’ll leave her to you, then, to get your revenge.”

I glanced over at Mother Ofburg, who, with her eyes, told me it was okay. I didn’t acknowledge her. I paid all my attention to Widow. “That’s generous of you.” I finished my meal and tried to leave it be, even though Mother Ofburg sat along with us.

“I’m curious as to how you will do it? She is a healer. I’m sure she will somehow try to stop you. Maybe play on your sensitive side.” Widow poked her fork at Mother Ofburg, who screamed as loud as she could with her mouth confined.

“I’ll think about it later. Beru may want to help, since she refused to heal him.” I couldn’t look at Mother Ofburg.

“Is that so? I love a good gossip.” Widow laughed out loud again with her evil laugh and poked Mother Ofburg harder with her fork. “I heard healers make good meals.”

“Too spicy for me.” I laughed for Widow’s benefit. “But she may be of use for Dag'draath when he is freed. He will need some healing. She has the most experience. If you didn’t want her dead.” I took a sip from my wine glass.

"You make a good point. But I am in the mood for some entertainment." Widow laughed again and brought her glass up for me to clank mine against hers.

"I'm up for either." I took a sip.

"Let's get back to Dag'draath and how we will free him. I need you to dreamwalk to him, preferably tonight. I can arrange for whatever you would need to do so." Widow leaned in. "I don't know why I'm so quiet. You won't live to tell our plans." Widow caressed Mother Ofburg's face with one of her poisonous tentacles.

Mother Ofburg leaned back as much as she could to get away from Widow. There wasn't enough room on Lynia for her to be that far.

"I can't do it on command. It will take time. Perhaps I could try later tonight when I'm tired. The wine may stop my ability . . ." I hadn't time to finish my sentence when her hand slapped my wine glass out of my hand.

"There. We can scratch that problem off." Her face was serious but then she broke out into huge fits of laughter. "If you could only see your face." She coughed from laughing so hard.

I laughed but was afraid it was too delayed. I wondered if she was also playing with me and if Mother Ofburg and I would both make it out of there alive. I'd tell her I could take her to the prison if she wanted to be with Dag'draath—to be his partner. I'd have a fighting chance to save Mother Ofburg if Widow needed to keep me around.

"I have an offer for you." I leaned in, and out of the corner of my eye, I could see Mother Ofburg's eyes widen as she shook her head frantically. I had to think for both of us now.

"Yes." Widow leaned in and exaggerated the word. Her eyebrow popped up as she waited for me to divulge my offer.

Just as I was about to tell her, I felt a pounding sensation in my head, as if someone was squeezing the sides of my head together. I grabbed onto my seat to steady myself and soon found myself being called to another dreamwalker—Runa.

"Are you out of your freaking mind!" she screamed at me as soon as I was pulled into her world. "What are you thinking? Are you even thinking at all?" Runa paced up and down and flailed her hands in the air.

I was on her floor, coughing and dealing with a pounding headache. "I had everything under control."

"You had nothing under control. How could you entertain conversing with Widow? She's well over your league. You don't actually think she was buying what you were selling do you?" Runa kept on her rant. I stayed quiet on the floor because I was weak, and I figured it would be best to let her go on before I spoke again.

“Do you have anything to say for yourself?” She stopped a foot in front of me.

I looked up to see if she was foaming from her mouth. She was not, so it was safe to try to conserve with her. “I needed to see why she took over my village. I have to find my family. She must have them.”

Runa sighed and crossed her arms. “Get up.”

I took her order and stood. I shook from weakness and the pounding headache that worsened with each scream. A chair appeared out of thin air, and I gladly sat on it. “It was the only option we had.”

Runa’s tone lowered. “And the others? Where are they now?”

“They’re in a cave. Waiting for me. If I don’t get back soon, they will go into the village.” I placed my hand over my eyes to shield them from the bright room.

“I’ll send a message.” Runa snapped her fingers.

I squinted as I looked up at her again. I had to get back there. Mother Ofburg was not safe with Widow, and each moment that passed was more deadly for her. I had to get back there, but how would I explain why I left? My head pounded even more as I tried to come up with a plan. Unless she’d already killed Mother Ofburg because I left.

“You’re not to do anything without talking to me.” Runa practically stomped her feet.

"Mother Ofburg. Did she die? I need to know," I begged.

Runa snapped her fingers, and Mother Ofburg appeared next to me.

"You played that a little too convincingly." Mother Ofburg pulled the ropes off her body.

"Mother Ofburg!" I screamed and hugged her as tightly as I could.

"I'm fine." She pushed me off her. "I just need a good bath."

I couldn't contain my excitement. I grabbed Mother Ofburg again, and she let me hug her. She wrapped her arms around me and rocked me back and forth. "It's alright. There, there." She patted my back.

"Thank you." I pulled away from Mother Ofburg and thanked Runa though my tears.

"We have a bigger issue to solve now. It can't wait any longer. We need to plug the prison. Many creatures have already escaped. I've managed to place a temporary shield over the prison, but it won't hold for much longer." Runa paced back and forth.

"Why hasn't Dag'draath found his way out, if other monsters have gotten through?" It didn't make any sense. They were his men. Surely, they would have brought him back with them.

"They must not want him out." Mother Ofburg brushed the dirt off her arms.

"I expect you're right. After staying two hundred and fifty years with the guy, they want to get fast and far away from him." Runa snapped her fingers, and a chair appeared. It was much more comfortable than ours.

"Can you do that?" Mother Ofburg appeared astonished.

"You'd know if I could." I sighed. My headache had subsided after my hug with Mother Ofburg. I expected she had healed me without even knowing.

"There is talk that these creatures also haven't let him out because they are stealing energy for him—enough so when he's ready, no one can defeat him. For now, he hides in the prison." Runa lay back in her chair and crossed her legs.

"And no monsters have gotten out in a while?" I wanted confirmation. The ones that broke out must be the reason for the raids.

"No. Not since I put the shield up. But it's weak. It won't last long. We need to find a solution now. It can't wait." Runa snapped her fingers, and a glass of wine appeared in each of our hands. "What?"

"I'm not complaining." Mother Ofburg took a drink of the wine.

"How do we plug the prison? We don't even know what will work." I sat at the edge of my seat. I was ready to help. I'd do anything to have the walls of the prison fixed so we could all go on with our lives. It had taken up too much of our time already. I was tired of thinking about it. Tired of living my life for the prison.

"You tell me. You broke into it and freed Beru." Runa leaned over so she was closer to me and waited for me to respond.

I didn't have a magical answer. It had been a fluke I even got Beru out of there and just barely. "There's no way to plug the prison. But we do have a key."

"A key?" Mother Ofburg looked confused. "I have never heard of this key."

"Not many people have." I paused, unsure if I should reveal Beru was the key. I feared they would hunt him down and his life would be retaken. But I also had no one else to turn to. "It's Beru."

Runa lifted an eyebrow and leaned back in her chair. A small smile curled the ends of her lips. "That's brilliant."

"It's not all said and done. He doesn't know that he's the key. He needs to find that within himself." I hoped they heard that last part. We couldn't hurry him along to fit our schedule.

"How can we nudge him?"

"He wants to go south. He's not sure why. That's where we were going before you called me, Mother Ofburg." No sooner had I finished my sentence than they both shared a knowing look. "What?"

"The prison is south."

My mouth opened. Why hadn't I realized that earlier? He was being called back to the prison by Dag'draath. That's why he didn't know why he was drawn there. Dag'draath would want to keep that a secret. Otherwise, Beru wouldn't go.

"Going south is a bad idea." Mother Ofburg shook her head. "They must know he is the key."

"Or maybe the prison is calling to him because he is the key," Runa added.

My head spun with all the new information. There was too much to think about and so little time. I hesitated to make the right decision. Iri and Sade wouldn't agree to go along to the prison, and I couldn't tell Beru anything. He had to find out he was the key himself. "What should I do?"

"You have to go. It's a bad idea, but you still have to go." Runa looked at Mother Ofburg, who nodded in agreement.

"This may be the only way to close the prison."

"He may need to be there again to know his mission," Runa added.

"This could do it. This could be the solution we were looking for." Mother Ofburg stood up.

"Are you prepared to leave him behind? If it means the prison will be safe again?"

I stood up quickly and walked away from them. I needed air badly. My lungs felt full, and I couldn't take enough breaths to fill them. I began to see stars and then everything went black. I could hear myself as I fell to the ground, but I couldn't feel any pain. Runa and Mother Ofburg ran to my side, calling my name.

I made my way back to the cave once I was well again. Runa told me to call on her before any decisions were made and I promised to do so. I arrived to find the cave was protected by Astor. The spiders had found them and were trying to get inside. Luckily, my body was already inside, so I could enter.

"We thought she made you tell her where we were." Astor hugged me.

"I'd never give you guys away." It made me uneasy they would think that of me.

"I never thought that." Beru leaned in and pulled me close to him. I let myself fall into his arms and relished the feeling of being close. He had a sweet scent, and his skin was moist against my cheek.

"I missed you," he whispered in my ear.

I pulled back from him, and before I could say anything, Sade pulled me in for her hug.

“Do you know how long you have been gone?” She looked at me, her voice conveying the concern her face couldn’t.

“No. Since this afternoon?” Time had wasted while I dreamwalked.

“Since yesterday. We were ready to bust in there to rescue you.” Sade laughed, but I knew she wasn’t joking. She was just happy I had returned in one piece.

“The forest filled with spiders not long after you left.” Iri came in for his hug.

“You should rest.” Beru pulled me aside and motioned for me to lie on the bed. “You look very tired.”

“I feel tired. My back aches, my muscles hurt, and my stomach is grumbling like I haven’t eaten in days.” I sat down on the bed and welcomed its comfort. It was lumpy, but I was ready to fall asleep any second.

“Not before you tell us what happened.” Sade sat at the end of the bed by my feet.

I told them everything I could remember, probably forgetting things as my eyes drooped from tiredness. I somehow drifted off to sleep while talking. My head hit the pillow, and I was done.

I woke up the next morning when the sun shone into the cave. There were spiders at the entrance, and they watched us as we slept.

"How long have they been there?" I looked at Sade, who was the only other person awake.

"For a while. Every now and then, they claw at the shield." Sade was preparing food for breakfast.

"Need any help?" I sat down next to her and the fire.

"You rest. I like a quiet morning, chopping things." She smiled.

I looked back at the three boys sleeping. Well, they were men, but they were my boys. I remembered that they thought I had told Widow where they were. It still stung to think about.

"You okay with your conversation with Runa? I know she can be hard at times." Sade passed me an apple to eat. "Last one. Saved for you."

I accepted it from her and took a bite. I hadn't eaten anything in days—at least my real self hadn't. I finished it up fast. "She's okay. She stopped me from making a big mistake with Widow."

"What's that?"

"Dreamwalking with Widow to the prison," I admitted as fast as I could, ashamed I had even thought of it.

"You're not serious. What would be the benefit of that?" She scrunched up her face in response to my carelessness.

"I wasn't actually going to do it, but I was going to offer it. I wanted to save Mother Ofburg." Sade wasn't there—she didn't understand the mood in that room. The carelessness of Widow.

"Mother Ofburg is with Runa?"

"I think so, or at least that's where I saw her last." I hoped Runa had the mind to keep her safe. I had half a mind to call on her and ask, if I wasn't feeling so drained.

Sade left me be while she finished prepping the food. I leaned my head on the side of the cave to rest. The dreamwalk had taken more out of me than I had anticipated.

"Here." Sade passed me some water. "Snap out of whatever has you."

"Thanks." I drank it back quickly and then grabbed one of the carrots she had cut up.

"So where do we go from here? We can't fight all these spiders."

"No, we can't." I took a deep breath and asked the question I didn't want to ask. "Do you know what lies south?"

"What do you mean?"

"The prison is south." I blurted it out.

Sade sat back and just looked at me. She scrunched her eyes up. I waited for her to reply. "Are we still going south?"

"I am. I can't ask it of you all. I don't want to tell Beru. I can't interfere with his journey to find out what he is." I looked over to make sure he was still asleep.

"Well, you're not going without me." Sade put it out there stubbornly.

I didn't have the mindset to argue with her. Plus, I didn't want anyone to hear. Sade was the only person I was telling for the moment.

I moved over, so my back was against the cave wall, and I gently placed my head back to rest it. I had no choice but to follow Beru to the south. I hoped whatever was calling him was good and not evil. My stomach groaned, more from the predicament at hand than from not eating.

I wasn't prepared to lose him. I couldn't lose him. I thought back to when we first met—to the feeling of knowing him already. The first time he smiled and when we touched.

"Aria?" Someone's voice poked through my consciousness as they sat next to me. I opened my eyes to see Beru.

"I was just napping." I stretched out.

“You seem really worried about something. Did you want to talk?” Beru passed me a plate of food Sade had prepared.

“I’m just overtired. I didn’t sleep well. And those guys are creepy.” I pointed to the spiders who kept watch over to us.

“Yeah, a little bit.” Beru smiled as he started on his breakfast.

“I’m thankful for the fire. It’s damp in here,” Iri grumbled as he took his serving. “I’ll have Astor’s too if he doesn’t get up.” Iri looked back at Astor, who was still covered in blankets and snoring away.

It was good to be back. To pretend like everything was normal and we were just hanging out in a cave.

“It won’t be long till Widow shows up. They’ve probably told her you’re here,” Iri sputtered between stuffing bread and eggs in his mouth.

“Yes, I’d bet you are right. She’s probably ordered them to take us back.” I looked at the shield, which appeared to be thinner than before. “How long will it hold up?”

“We won’t run out of food, that’s for sure.” Sade piled more food on Beru’s and Iri’s plates.

“Can we go further in the cave? Is there another way out?”

"Not this one. We can go in further, but they'll just come in after us once the shield fades. We couldn't see through it when he first put it up. They are out there waiting for it to come down. Astor's not fast enough to put up another one before they come in." Sade finally sat down to eat her own plate of food.

"Can you dreamwalk us out of here?" Iri laughed.

He may have been joking, but I had been able to dream port myself out of fearful situations before. We had the shield up, so I could practice, but I was still very weak. "I might be able to. Once I'm stronger."

"How long will that take?" Sade asked.

"After that shield comes down." I looked at the front of the cave.

"Save me first." Astor joined us. "I weigh less too." He poked Iri, who was the largest, in the stomach, which was like solid rock. Iri grunted at him.

"Where would we go?" Sade wanted to know.

"Somewhere close, just out of the spider range. It would take less energy then." I started to plan in my head how I could do it. One dream port I could manage. If we could get one more day out of the shield.

"Now that Mother Ofburg is safe, are we heading south again?" Astor pointed in the original direction we had been heading.

"I'm not sure." I leaned on my side to conserve my energy.

"Okay, everyone, let's leave her alone. She's exhausted and needs a break from all our questions." Sade practically swatted them away from me.

"Thank you." I closed my eyes and rested while I listened to their morning chatter, pretending everything was normal. I wondered if we'd all stay together when this was over and live side by side. Maybe Beru and I would marry. I smiled but knew I was so tired I was being silly.

I must have fallen asleep because when I woke up, I had a severe cramp in my side from how I was leaning. Sade, Iri, and Astor were playing a game quietly and Beru was still beside me.

"Hey, beautiful." He smiled at me, and I couldn't help but smile back.

"What are you still doing sitting by me?" I sat up and stretched.

"I might like watching you sleep." Beru looked away with a smile.

"That might just be the sweetest thing someone has ever said to me." I leaned my head back on the stone and watched him. My eyes still burned from needing more sleep, but I wanted to stay awake and talk to him.

“I find that hard to believe.” Beru moved his hand over and rubbed his pinky on mine.

We just stared into each other`s eyes, with the sound of our friends playing a game in the background. My eyes wanted to drift off to sleep again, but I fought against them. It may be the only memory like it that we shared. Our lives hung in the balance, and our futures were unknown. Nothing was guaranteed except the moment.

“It’s getting thinner.” Sade stood up as one of the spiders leaned against the shield, and it moved inward.

We all got up and walked over to the shield. They pressed on it, and it moved. More spiders accumulated on the other side. They begin to push on each other to see how far the shield would bend into the cave.

“This is not good.” The shield flexed again, and Sade pushed it back out. “How about that teleporting thing again, Aria?”

I’d have to try. Soon, the spiders would break through and take us back to Widow. At least some of us. Others would be killed. I needed to get us out of there and fast, but I could barely walk. I leaned against the cave wall and felt a dizzy spell coming on. Everything went black again, but someone caught my fall.

I heard their voices first. "We have to get her up."

"They're going to break through."

When I opened my eyes, everything was fuzzy. Soon, the blackness faded to stars and then blurry images.

"She's opening her eyes." I heard Sade say from somewhere in the cave.

I moaned, not able to think hard enough to put words together. Someone lifted me and placed a pillow under my head. The back of someone's hand touched my forehead.

"Here's some water." I heard Iri. Someone brought the cup to my lips, and I took a sip.

I opened my eyes again, and I could see it more clearly. Everyone around me looked worried. I rolled my head over to see the shield was almost ready to break through. A sense of urgency and inner strength came over me. I pulled myself to a seated position.

"Drink some more." Iri practically took a tooth out with his persistence.

I drank from the cup and then pushed it away. "I'm fine. I just need a minute." I scooted back to the cave wall as everyone looked at me like I was some wild animal they had captured.

"I don't mean to sound insensitive, but do you think we could teleport now?" Astor leaned in and nodded at the spiders outside of the cave.

We had to leave soon or else the worst would happen. I wasn't sure how I'd have enough energy to carry them all through a teleport and stopped myself from thinking I'd have to choose.

"Do you need a minute? No pressure." Sade's facial expression said otherwise.

There was too much going on inside my head. I closed my eyes to try to sort it out, but extreme exhaustion set in quickly. It felt like someone was standing on my chest, and I couldn't breathe properly. I started to take larger breaths, but they didn't reach deep into my lungs.

"You have to relax. You're having a panic attack." Beru placed his hand on my shoulder and motioned with his hand for how I should be breathing. I looked him in the eyes and kept that gaze and started to feel calmer. "Just focus on me."

I nodded at him and followed his breathing exercises until I felt well enough to breathe on my own without panicking. “I don’t know what came over me.” My face flushed with embarrassment over my weakness.

“Don’t worry about anything. We have time.” Sade rubbed my leg.

I looked back at the shield, and the spiders were able to push it in a good foot. We didn’t have time to spare. We had to get out of the cave fast, no matter how I was feeling.

“I’ll need to take your energy. I don’t have enough of mine.” I reached out and grabbed Beru and Sade’s hands. “Form a circle.”

Iri and Astor joined in, everyone holding hands. “I’ll need to take more than before, and even then, I can’t guarantee that I will be able to do it.”

“If you can’t, you must go and take Beru. The prison needs to be closed, for everyone’s sake,” Sade stated.

“What do you mean?” Astor flipped his head to Sade. “I’m not staying here.”

“No one is staying here. We are all going.” I reassured them something I couldn’t. “I want everyone to focus on leaving this cave.” I made eye contact with each of them and then I closed my eyes and tried to pull energy from the circle. At first, nothing happened. I had to push all my feelings aside so I could tap into the pure power inside us all.

"It's not working," Astor whispered.

I opened my eyes in time to see Sade as she slapped him. Iri grumbled under his breath something I could barely make out. Beru remained solid as a rock in his trance.

"It's going to take me some time. I'm not as fast as I normally am, and this is something I've never done." I was pleading with Astor. His inability to focus could sink us before we even started.

We all got back into our positions, and I tried to clear my mind again. The pressure built up and I dropped my hands. I couldn't do it. I was too tired. "I'm sorry." I leaned over and let my head fall into my hands and cried.

"You can do this." Beru wrapped his arms around me and rocked me back and forth.

Then Sade moved closer and put her hand on me. Then Iri and Astor. Something in the pit of my stomach stirred, and I felt the energy begin to build up inside me.

"Let's try again." I sat up and wiped my tears. I had something to build on now. We all held hands, and I was able to access their energy. It wasn't strong, but it began to build. "Think about being on the Island. The sand on your toes, sitting back in the sun," I instructed them.

My hands started to tingle as I received more energy from them. I pushed the sounds of the spiders as they scraped at the shield out of my mind and only thought about being in the temple. The fresh air that flowed through the open windows and the cold floor on my tired, hot feet.

I remembered sitting in the hot water spring. The water washing over me as my muscles relaxed. How I wanted to be back there more than anything with my friends, away from harm. I squeezed their hands and dug deep down inside to find the energy I knew I needed to be able to teleport them all.

My hair started to stand up from the energy I was collecting. I felt little jolts of shock from each hand I held run up my arms. The hair all over my body stood up straight as I sucked in all the energy I could.

Something started to happen. I could feel the ground move underneath me. It rumbled as I was lifted above it, but it was only me. Beru and Sade were still on the cave's floor. It was as if they were anchoring me there. It wasn't going to work. I couldn't take them all at the same time.

I opened my eyes, and I fell to the ground with a large thud. "It's not working." The sounds of the spiders outside only infuriated me more. *Why can't I do this?* They were all depending on me. This was a life or death mission, and I was failing them. Soon, the shield would break, and we were no match for the number of spiders camped outside.

"Do one at a time. Start with Beru. Let's go." Sade slapped her hands together and stood up. She pushed Iri and Astor back and nodded at Beru to take both of my hands.

'But what . . ." I tried to protest.

Sade interrupted me. "One at a time. You'll come back."

Beru grabbed onto my hands and closed his eyes, not giving me much choice in the matter. I closed my eyes as well and focused on the Island. I sucked in his energy, and it overcame me. His energy was hot and seductive and showed me his soul. It was pure and sweet. My body started to sweat, but soon, we both lifted off the floor and were being teleported.

I could feel my feet touch the grass and my eyes flew open. Beru and I were in the forest, far enough away to be safe. I was shocked it had worked, and I still had enough energy to travel back alone.

"You did it," Beru yelled as he picked me up in his arms and swung me around in the air. "You have to go back now. I'll scout the area and find a safe place to bunk down in."

I nodded and quickly got back into my trance. The sooner I did, the easier it would be to teleport. I was back in the cave in no time.

“I knew it! Is it safe?” Sade jumped up and down, laughing.

“Yes. Let’s do this quickly. Who’s next?” I looked between the three of them. They would have to choose.

Sade looked at Iri, “Astor.”

Iri nodded in agreement. Astor grabbed my hands. He wanted to get out of there quickly.

“No, the shield will come down. He’s last.” The thought hadn’t occurred to me before. I grabbed Sade’s hands before she could reject my comment and stole her energy. We quickly transported to where Beru was.

“Aria. That was not the plan.” Sade pulled her hands away, clearly shocked at what had just happened.

“I’m going back for Iri.” I didn’t have time to argue, and I was losing energy each trip. I closed my eyes and was back in the cave.

“Astor this time.” Iri pushed Astor toward me, and he tried to grab my hands, but I refused.

“No. You will die, Iri. This way, we are all safe. Don’t waste any more time. I’m losing energy. I need to hurry to make it back to Astor.” I held my hands out to him as Astor looked back at Iri, panicked.

"I can't stay here alone." Astor stomped his feet on the cave floor and began to cry. "I can't, Aria."

"You can. I will only be gone a few minutes. You can do this. Iri, let's go." I walked over to him, and he reluctantly looked at my hands.

Astor rushed toward us, but I was able to teleport before he reached us.

We joined Sade and Beru, but I fell to the ground. My energy was almost depleted, and I wasn't confident I could make a round trip again. They all rushed to my side.

"Take my energy." Iri held out his hand. "Take it all."

"That's not how this works." My eyes filled with tears.

"Can you go and come back safely?" Sade knelt beside me.

"I'm going to try." I nodded to her, and she began to cry.

She knew how big of a risk it was.

I closed my eyes and dug my hands in Lynia's soil as I tried to harness her energy. It was different than human, monster, or healer energy. It may be what saved the mission, but I could only touch rock in the cave, so I wasn't sure how I would get back.

I felt myself come into cool darkness, and I knew I was back in that cave. I barely had time to open my eyes before Astor grabbed me. "Where were you?" he cried. "I thought you were never coming back."

"I'd never leave you here, old friend." I rubbed his back and looked over at the shield.

It was beginning to deteriorate.

One of the spiders had poked through, and his spindles were stuck. It was only a matter of time before he was able to rip through it, and it would get a lot smaller in there.

"Okay, last one." I closed my eyes as I wrapped my arms around him. I tried to tap into his energy—his magic—but he was too scared and had closed himself up.

The spiders were making progress with the rip in the shield. They pushed and pulled on it as they tried to make it bigger. I tried to ignore it, but my fear set in. Not for me but for Astor. Widow would want them to bring me to her. She would do away with Astor.

I had to get us out of there.

I heard feet scurry on the cave floor. First, they had broken through. I opened my eyes as a giant spider was almost on top of us. I held up my hand and grabbed onto him. I closed my eyes and wished to be with Beru.

The sound changed. It made me almost dizzy. I wasn't sure what was happening but knew neither one of us were hurt. I opened my eyes and saw we were in the middle of being teleported. It worked. I used the energy of the spider.

It took us longer to reach them, but when we did, there were lots of hugs and tears. We had all made it to safety, and I could finally relax and regain my strength.

I turned away from my friends for a moment to myself. My happiness plummeted as I noticed a plume of smoke far off in the forest.

Widow had set the village on fire because she couldn't have me.

I felt water on my cheek. I didn't have the energy to find out where it was coming from. I stood motionless as I gazed at the rising smoke. I couldn't hear the wind in the trees or my friends as they spoke not far behind me. The silence was deafening, as if I were swimming underwater.

I looked back at Iri, Astor, and Sade. They were celebrating escaping a near-death experience. They hadn't noticed what we left behind. I wanted to scream at them to stop celebrating. That people were dead, possibly my family. I couldn't speak. I opened my mouth, and nothing came out.

Sade noticed me first. She pointed at me to get their attention. She called to me, but I couldn't hear what she was saying. I was still underwater.

They came to me with worried looks on their faces. I pointed to the smoke and watched their expressions change from happiness to remorse just like mine had.

Sade lifted her hand to her mouth while Iri and Astor stared at the smoke as if they were mesmerized. Beru looked away. I turned back as the smoke became darker and more widespread.

Sade wrapped her arms around me, and I buried my head in her shoulder and cried. We had seen much destruction since we began working together, but it was harder when it was the village you worked in. People you saw every day for years. Your family.

"We'll stop her. I promise you that, Aria," Sade whispered in my ear.

I held on to her.

Beru joined in with our hug, then Iri and Astor. We all rocked in the wind and took time to be in the moment and feel for the first time in a long time. We had just been moving from one disaster to another.

"Can I join?" A voice interrupted our protected hug.

We broke apart, and as Iri moved to the side, Mother Ofburg appeared.

I ran to her with open arms, and we embraced. I needed her more than anyone. She would know what to do and how to handle everything. I had made such a mess of it.

"Now, now. Widow would have done it anyway. This is not your fault." Mother Ofburg rubbed the tears off my cheeks. "There's no time for crying now."

“Tell me what to do.” I pulled away from her and waited for all the right answers. I’d do whatever she wanted me to do.

“I think you’re a better judge of what should be done.”

Mother Ofburg greeted everyone. I gathered myself together while they spoke. She was right. I had to lead the group. I couldn’t fall apart. We’d just beat an impossible situation. I couldn’t let them down by giving up.

We had to continue our mission.

“The town is lost, I’m afraid. I can’t say for sure who made it out and who was trapped. I only know who hid with me.” Mother Ofburg looked toward me with sad eyes.

I knew she was talking about my family. Vinsha was in the dome and certainly lost. I prayed my brother and their baby were safe, and that was the reason they were not caught with her.

“What happened? When Aria left, they seemed content with holding people hostage.” Sade probed, trying to get more information.

“I’m guessing it was because she had Aria but then she lost her. But I can’t say for sure.” Mother Ofburg waved her hands. It was difficult for her to talk about.

“Did she know we were in the cave?” Iri took his turn with Mother Ofburg.

"That I don't know. When I got back from my visit with Runa, the fires had already started. It was chaotic. People were running everywhere. I took who I could, and we hid. I made a break for it when it got dark." Mother Ofburg's hands shook as she explained what she had seen.

"Widow won't stop." Beru stood off to the side, not quite close enough to partake in our conversation.

"He's right. She won't. She will move on to another town and do the same. And then there will be more monsters set free. Lynia will not be safe until the prison is fixed."

I put my head down, I knew what we had to do. We had to leave the village behind and continue south. Beru needed to figure out that he was the key. I was ready to scream the news at him, but that would compromise his journey.

"Beru and Aria, you must continue on. You need to hurry." Mother Ofburg reached for our hands.

I knew what she was going to do. As a healer, she was the best reader of people. She knew more in a touch than spending twenty years with someone. She could also give us some of her healing powers to use later if we needed. But that also meant she would lose some of her resources, and they may never come back.

"We need to go south." I glanced at Beru, who was already looking at me.

"I agree. I still don't know why, but I feel like that's the answer."

"Then you must go. All of you." Mother Ofburg stood back and extended her hand to the rest of our group.

We joined hands and had a moment of silence. I felt Mother Ofburg's energy as she dispersed it amongst us. I tried to pull away, but she held firm, and I gave in. I closed my eyes as tears fell.

She was giving us her gift and potentially her life.

I kissed her cheek as we broke apart. "Thank you."

"You're young and have much of your life. I'm old and used up, my dear. I see nothing but good things for you." Mother Ofburg hugged me.

"So, south it is. I'll gather up what little we have. We can find more along the way." Sade called the boys together.

"I wanted to talk with you alone." Mother Ofburg pulled me off for a walk into the woods, away from the others.

"I need all the advice you can give."

“He’s a good man. I know you have had your doubts and so have I. His energy is good. You will do well to trust him.” Mother Ofburg stopped at the water’s edge.

A wave of relief washed over me. I had fought hard with myself the past few months about Beru’s character and potential. “I’m afraid I’ve ruined any chance of that happening.” I hung my head low. There wasn't enough time to tell her why.

“Forgiveness. First with yourself, and in time, with him.” Mother Ofburg put her arm around my shoulder.

I noticed her healing touch was gone. She had given it all to us.

She smiled down on me. “I’ll be fine.”

I looked out onto the water. It was so peaceful. I wanted to remember the moment for as long as I had.

“I’ll give it all back when I return,” I promised her.

Mother Ofburg smiled knowingly, but she didn’t challenge me. “He’s the one for you. Don’t fight it, child. I have seen. You will be happy with no other.”

“I’ve felt it too. Tried not to.” I half smiled. I didn’t feel worthy of him most of the time.

“Let down your wall. It will be important for this trip. Get to know him better,” Mother Ofburg urged.

Mother Ofburg knew more than I did, that was for sure. Even if she had never loved a man before. Or perhaps she had. “Any more advice I can take from you on this trip?”

“Don’t be so hard on yourself. You did what you thought had to be done. It didn’t come from a place of evil—it came from your heart.” She nodded as she looked off into the distance.

“I love you. I always have.” I fought back the tears. It had hurt so much to see her angry with me. She was like a mother to me for so long. I lost part of myself when she threw me out that day.

“We all make mistakes. Even me. That day was my mistake. Grief holds you hostage at times, and it’s impossible to see in front of you. Sometimes, it’s scary to think ahead in a different world. I trust you will forgive my lack of judgment in that weak moment.”

I hugged her hard. “Already forgotten.”

“Then, it’s time. You must gather your troops and head out. It will only get worse, quickly.”

I nodded my head and gave her one last hug. “Where will you go?”

“Don’t worry about me. I will find my place.”

I walked back to my crew and left her by the water. They had already gathered the little we had and were waiting for me to return to them.

“Is she coming with us?” Sade gestured to Mother Ofburg by the water.

“No, I think she has a different journey ahead of her.” I gave her once last glance. “Let’s head out. We have a long walk ahead of us.”

We started out. Sade and Iri walked ahead of me, followed by Astor, and then Beru and I. No one spoke as we prepared ourselves for the next mission. The stakes had risen, and we’d just lost a huge battle. It would take time to get over, and we didn’t have time. We needed to push all the insecurities aside to seal the prison for good.

We walked until darkness set in. We left the road and made a shelter deep in the woods, careful to keep our fire small in case of rogue ur’gels finding us. We didn’t know who was on our side anymore or how far the war had spread.

Sade and I settled in and gathered the little food we had into a soup so it would spread further. The boys gathered wood for the night and set up a place to sleep. Most of us kept to our tasks and avoided speaking. I stirred the water in the pot while Sade dropped in vegetables and herbs.

"It won't be the worst meal we've had." Sade sighed as the last little bit hit the water. "I hope to come across civilization tomorrow."

"Maybe a farmer's field. I'd rather not steal, but I don't want to risk being seen." I stirred the soup.

"Do you think you will see Mother Ofburg again?"

At first, I didn't answer. I wanted to believe I would, but I knew most likely that would not be the case. I settled on saying, "I hope so."

"I'm glad, anyway, that you sorted things out with her. I know that was important to you." Sade sat back on the grass and arranged out our bowls, even though it would be a while before the soup was ready.

"Me too," I muttered, not ready to talk about her.

"I know what she did."

I knew what she meant, and I was happy not to be the only one to carry that burden. I nodded and turned back to the pot. I didn't need to stir it constantly, but it gave me something to do, and I didn't have to think about anything else.

Sade closed her eyes. "I'm dreaming about walking on the sand. Being back on the Island."

"It was pretty special." I was happy for the change of subject. I needed to be happy and think positively. It could save my life later.

“The food!” Sade groaned. “I’d live there just for the food.”

“You’d live there?” Her comment surprised me. She hated people.

“I would. I think I would. It’s been the best place that I have been in a long time. I could get used to working for Captain Rose.”

“And have a normal life?” I quizzed her.

“Yeah, I’d like a normal life after this. I’m getting old.” Sade laughed. “I’m about ready to retire.”

“Oh, come on.” I threw a small stick at her. “You wouldn’t know what to do with yourself if you retired.”

Her comment didn’t sit right with me. There was a chance she wouldn’t make it through the next mission. A chance none of us would make it through.

“I’d enjoy myself. You should think about it too. After all of this is done.” Sade waved her hand in a circle.

I smiled back at her. I was not as optimistic about surviving as she was. I was living day to day. I wasn’t afraid to die anymore. It was a side effect of living life and not something to dwell on. But seeing Sade have a plan for the future made me think more cautiously. I wanted her to have that dream, but I knew it would be slim.

As the others arrived back with wood and supplies for bedding, the conversation slowed. We were all exhausted from teleporting.

"Can I ask the obvious question? The one everyone is too scared to ask?" Astor pointed his spoon up in the air.

I rolled my eyes. He liked to stir the pot. I didn't want to know his question, as I was sure neither did anyone else.

"No," Sade replied almost immediately.

"Come on," Astor begged.

"Go ahead. I'm guessing it's about me." Beru sat back from the circle into the darkness.

"*He* said it's okay to ask." Astor pointed to Beru. His comment was met with sighing and silence. No one wanted to waste any energy arguing.

"Why are we all going south when Beru doesn't know why? It seems arrogant to me." Astor placed his hand on his chest.

"Here we go," Sade leaned over and whispered. "Don't even bother to answer that one."

"He has a right to ask it." Beru brought his makeshift chair closer to the fire. "I'm blindly leading you all. It's okay to say it." Beru looked at each one of us. "I'm not afraid to talk about it."

"We are following Aria." Sade made a strong statement.

Iri finally spoke up. "And Beru."

His comment stunned me. He appeared to be angry about not knowing as well. He'd held it in very well, so I'd had no indication he was upset.

"And I thank you for that. Couldn't do this without any of you. I know it's a lot to ask, and I don't ask it lightly." His gaze never broke from us. "I've also not been myself, so seeing past that and still coming along means a lot to me."

"Why can't you remember? Who told you to go south? That doesn't make sense to me." Astor piled the questions on.

"It's a feeling I have. I need to go there. I can't stop thinking I need to go. The closer we get, the more I feel the pull." Beru pounded his chest.

I looked at Astor to try and give him a look to keep quiet, but he was too deep in this conversation. "What if it's something evil? That's the thing—we have no idea what it is." He stood up and preached to us all. "Doesn't anyone else think this is all crazy?"

"That's enough, Astor." I stood up as well. "If you don't want to come, then don't. And that goes for anyone else. No one is forced to go on."

I left the group and walked off into the woods. I ran for a bit so no one could follow me. I should be resting for the journey. Instead, I was fighting with my closest friends to try to defend Beru. And I knew they partially thought it was because I was falling in love with him.

I wasn't following him because of that. I didn't know if the pull had anything to do with the key, but it was all we had. There wasn't time to think or make another plan. I lay down in the tall grass. I thought I would cry, but there were no more tears left.

I was pathetic with all the crying I was doing. I chuckled to myself. Why was I so emotional? I closed my eyes and placed my hands on Lynia. I needed her energy and wisdom to get me through. I dug my hands into her soil. "Am I on the right path?" I didn't expect her to answer. I'd have to find the answer within. Something I was not capable of at that moment.

I lay there and listened to the wind move the tall grass around me. It reminded me of my childhood, playing in the fields with my brothers. I wondered if they were okay.

I swore I'd come back for them once it was all over. I'd make sure nothing hurt them again.

I drifted off into a deep sleep.

The sun woke me the next morning. As soon as I realized where I was, I jumped up and made my way back to the camp. They'd be worried about me being gone for so long. I ran as fast as I could.

I made it back to the campfire, but no one was there. I went over to where our beds were prepared and again, no one was there. Had they left without me?

"They've gone out to look for you." Astor peeked out from behind the tree.

"And you've hidden behind a tree?" I looked at him oddly.

"You did run rather fast into the camp. I wasn't even sure if it was you." Astor came out and sat by the campfire. "Are you all right?"

"I'm fine. I just needed to get away." I looked around for any trace of breakfast that was left behind.

"I'm sorry about last night. I don't know what came over me. I don't think sometimes." Astor half looked my way.

"You started quite the fight," I responded.

"You didn't see the half of it. It got worse when you left."

I didn't want to ask about it. I finally had a good night's sleep, and I wanted to put it all behind us. We should have left already.

"There she is," Sade called as she exited the woods. She ran toward me and knelt. "We were worried. You're never gone that long."

"I know. I fell asleep. I needed it." I half smiled at her.

Iri and Beru exited the woods as well. They looked like they had been up all night looking for me.

"She's fine. No thanks to you." She pointed at Beru.

Iri grunted in acknowledgment. The dynamic was different. I certainly had missed a lot while I was away. Beru remained quiet.

Sade baited him. "You're the reason all of this is happening."

Beru looked at the ground and didn't budge or respond to Sade. She walked over to him and stood an inch away from his face. She was ready to fight. "Say something. Prove it's not your fault." Sade pounded her fist on his chest.

Beru looked up at her, and his eyes closed. He wasn't going to let her get away with pushing him. Iri noticed the change in his face and walked over to them as he cracked his knuckles.

"Guys, it's okay. Aria is back now." Astor jumped up, likely feeling guilty at what he had caused.

"Astor is right. We have to put this aside and get going." I stood up and walked over to them, ready to put myself between Beru and Sade. I had never seen her so mad before.

"It's not all right. Beru should have left last night," Sade yelled.

"Why?" I tried to push myself between them but neither budged.

"For wasting our time," Sade yelled. She flexed her fist and held it back as if she was going to take a swing. I swiftly jumped on her, and we fell to the ground. I struggled to hold her down as she fought to stand up.

"Sade, stop it!" I climbed on top of her and finally managed to control her by straddling her. "What is wrong with you?" I yelled.

"Let her up." Iri tapped my shoulder.

"No. Just stop this. All of you!" I screamed, out of breath from trying to contain Sade. "We won't fight each other."

I looked around at each of them. I wasn't sure if Iri would rush Beru or not. Astor stood off to the side, not wanting to get into any physical alteration. Sade finally gave up struggling with me.

"I'm with Aria on this." Astor held his hand up like we were taking a vote.

"He needs to go." Sade got her wind back and tried to get me off her. Iri stood back, ready to intervene if it got physical.

Sade tried to wiggle her way out from under me. She flipped me over on my back. "You can't beat the mentor." She got up and made a run for Beru.

Iri stopped her before she made it to him. He wrapped his arms around her as she struggled to get past him. "It's over," Iri repeated until she stopped fighting him

"Wait!" Beru stepped forward.

Everyone stopped what they were doing to look toward him. He closed his eyes, and both of his hands were on his head. "I remember something."

I got up from the ground and made my way to him. The others stayed where they were. "What do you mean?"

"I hid something." He squinted as if he was trying to recall something.

"Where?" I grabbed his elbow.

"In the prison. That's what has been calling me."

"Are you sure?" I grabbed both of his arms. I wanted to hug him. We were one step closer to him realizing he was the key.

"Yes." Beru had tears in his eyes.

"Listen up." I turned from him back to the group that surrounded us. "We need to pull ourselves together. Nobody has to come on this mission. If you want to leave, raise your hand."

I looked around at everyone, but they all avoided eye contact with me and didn't raise their hands. I had to get us all on the same page. We needed to leave behind all the arguments when we left today.

"Raise your hand if you are coming with us."

Sade raised her hand first, then Astor and Iri. They looked ashamed at how far their argument had gone. A good night's sleep would do everyone some good.

"This is hard. On all of us. We have to stick together. There can be no more second-guessing. If you're coming, you're all in." I stepped back so I wasn't in front of Beru anymore.

"I'm sorry. I don't know what came over me." Sade offered her hand to Beru for a truce, and he didn't hesitate to shake it.

Iri was next.

"I started this all." Astor stood up and hugged Beru. "Sorry, brother."

We all took a seat at the campfire once the apologies were said. Sade scrambled a few eggs with what we had left and divided it amongst us.

"What do you think it could be?" I hoped more had come to Beru since his revelation.

"Something I wanted to keep safe from them. But I'm not sure what." Beru leaned over, his elbows on his knees.

"What made you remember?" Sade spoke up.

"The fighting, I think. It felt like déjà vu." Beru rubbed his hand over his face.

"At least it was good for something." Sade smiled as she tried to make light of the conversation.

"I'm sorry I ever brought it up." Astor joined in.

"Well, if you hadn't set off the chain of events, I'm not sure I would have realized. At least we have something to go on now." Beru sat back.

"I'm just happy for food." Iri took the plate Sade handed him.

"Savor it. This is the last of it." She passed the other plates around to the group. "If you hid it, it must be something valuable to them. I wonder if they knew you had it?"

"I don't think so. Life would have been much harder for me in there if they did. There are only a few places I could have hidden it well. If we split up to look for it, that could save us some time."

"Good plan." I dug into my food and wondered what he could have hidden. Was it the key we had been looking for? Or something else. Something from the war?

"How would you have hidden it?" Iri shoveled another bite into his mouth.

"I'm not sure. I think I would have likely buried it. Somewhere in the sand maybe." He shook his head and tried to recall where he could have hidden something.

I was thankful for the breakthrough. We were one step closer to finding what was calling him. Whatever it was would help us seal the prison and make him remember who he really was. I finished off my plate and placed it in the wash bin.

"It's time. We leave for the south together as a team." I held my first up in the air. "Who is with me?"

They all followed with their fists. We were one step closer to fixing the prison and ending the madness that had escaped.

We opted for more rest before we left. We were about a day's walk away from the prison, and it would be our last chance to get some sleep before we got there. It was well needed with the irritableness going around.

I got up earlier than the rest of them, having slept most of the night. I walked down to the water's edge and found Beru sitting by himself. I sat down beside him. "I didn't realize you were up. Shouldn't you be getting sleep in while you can?"

"I've slept enough." He held up a string of fish. "Besides, I needed my peace offering."

"I can't fight that." I smiled, looking out over the water.

"Thank you for sticking up for me. I know you were going up against your family." Beru hugged his knees to his chest.

"I believe in you. You know more about that prison than any of us."

“I hate that you were brought into this, even though you saved me.”

I smiled at his sentiment. I wasn’t sorry. I’d have never met him otherwise. My life changed because of him, and I was proud of that. I learned to be the fighter I never knew I had in me.

“It’s how it’s meant to be.” I leaned over and nudged him teasingly.

Beru pulled me closer to him and kissed me. The few seconds before his lips met mine, I questioned if I should stop him or pull away, but my body betrayed me and leaned in. His soft, wet lips caressed mine until finally, he pulled away.

“I’ve wanted to do that for a while.” Beru brought his hand to my face and moved my hair away. “You’re beautiful, Aria.”

I was stunned. *Say something!* I yelled at myself in my head. “So are you,” I managed to finally say. My face flushed. How could I call a man beautiful? I shook my head as I pulled away from him.

“Not something I would call myself. But I will take that from your lips.” Beru grabbed my face and pulled me in for another kiss. It was just as sweet as the first and left me breathless. “I’m taking advantage.”

"No, really. You're not. I wish I were as brave as you."

"You're the bravest person I know." Beru squeezed my hand.

"You might not say that if you knew me better." I pulled away from him and leaned back, letting the sun hit my face.

"I'm sure I would. Do you think I don't know you?" Beru appeared intrigued by this new challenge.

"Maybe." I teased him.

Beru lay on his side next to me. I retreated to my back, and we casually stared at each other. I had never had a significant other, but he had been married. I wondered if he compared us. If, when he kissed me, he was thinking of her.

They didn't separate because they hated each other. She was killed. Did his love die with her? Or was I a different love? I didn't know. I didn't know how to love him as I should. I didn't have much luck with men.

"What are you thinking?" His hand caressed my face.

"Ramblings." I laughed uncomfortably. I liked his touch, but I didn't know how to receive it. I feared I was awkward when it came to romance.

"I want to hear these ramblings." Beru leaned in and gently kissed my cheek.

Normally, I would have stopped such touches, but it may be our last day. I let him in like Mother Ofburg suggested. *I will not stop this. I will not stop this.*

"Come on. Let our worlds collide. What is in that pretty little head?" Beru kissed my forehead.

"You ever think past all of this? What you want to do?" I rolled over to face him.

"I guess. Sometimes."

"Do you see me in your sometimes?" I brushed some sand off his cheek.

"Always." He grew serious. "You're always on my mind. No matter what I do."

He leaned in for another kiss. This time, he started on my forehead and gently kissed his way down to my lips.

My head felt dizzy, so I lay back in the sand. He placed his arm across me and leaned into me.

"Do you think about me?" Beru placed his forehead on mine. The heat from his body warmed any coldness I had inside.

"Always." I laughed. It was awkward to talk that way. It felt unnatural, yet I wanted to learn how to do it right.

"When this is all over, I want to take you away. I don't care where we go. I just want to be alone with you for a while." Beru played with the button on my shirt.

My face flushed as I thought of what could possibly be going through his mind in that moment.

“Aria! Beru!” Sade called our names from back at the camp. I pushed Beru away and jumped up quickly, afraid she would see him on top of me and think something of it.

“W … we should go,” I stuttered as I pointed my thumb in her direction.

“You go first.” Beru lay back in the sand. “Take these.” He handed me the fish and winked. “They can be your alibi.”

I smiled and then ran as fast as I could up the hill to the campsite. I prayed Sade hadn’t seen us. I’d know right away if she did. She would have a million questions for me.

“We have fish!” I held them up in front of my reddened face.

“I love you!” Sade folded her hands in front of her and then grabbed the fish from my hands. She ran them past her nose to smell, and she smiled ear to ear. “Help me get them ready for breakfast.”

I nodded and ran past her to grab the grill to put over the fire.

“Wait. Why is your face so red?” She stood with her hands on her hips and shot a cocked eyebrow my way.

"The sun. Why?" I kept busy lighting the fire.

"Hmm . . ."

"I got a few more," Beru called as he joined us. He held up four more fish. "That lake is stocked."

"Put them here." Sade slapped the rock she had used to prepare the other fish. "We will all eat like kings at our last supper."

"Sade, stop acting like we are going to die today." I gently nudged her.

Sade shrugged and chopped off the fish heads with one swing. "It's fifty-fifty these days."

I ignored her morbid comment, stoked the fire to get it hot, and placed the grill on top of it. "It's ready." My mouth watered as she added the fish.

"I smelled food, and I came running." Astor joined us. Iri was not far behind as he rubbed the crud out of his eyes.

"Fish. Aria and Beru caught them." She looked back and forth between Beru and me. I ignored her and focused on the food she was cooking. My stomach grumbled as the smell of frying fish filled the air. We had only had vegetables and fruit for so long.

"Have you had anything else come to you?" Sade flipped the fish.

“I remembered some things about the final battle.” Beru rubbed his stomach.

Iri seemed intrigued with this new information. “Like what?”

“I was on an errand for Onen Suun.” Beru stretched out his legs. “He knew he had to imprison Dag’draath. But he didn’t have enough power.”

“He was that strong, even then?” Astor’s voice dropped in awe.

“He was. Onen Suun sent me after a stone: Death`s Breath. It was rumored to have immense power. With that stone, Onen Suun would have enough power to put a spell on the prison.” Beru stopped—it seemed painful for him to remember.

“Was he a wizard like me?” Astor became more intrigued with the story.

“No. But the spell created the prison.”

I interrupted him. “Is the stone what is calling you back?”

“I think so, but I can’t be sure until we find whatever it was that I hid. It’s becoming clearer to me now.”

“Did you find the stone?” Astor was deep into the story now.

“Yes. It wasn’t easy, but in the end, I did find it.”

"What happened next?" Astor's eyes were big. Sade and Iri shared a smiled at Astor's enthusiasm.

"It's blurry, but I remember having to pass different tests. I was in the middle of one when we were attacked. I'm guessing that's when I hid it somewhere." Beru shook his head as he tried to remember what happened.

"So, he never had the stone when he made the prison?" I had always been interested in how the prison came to be. This was the first I had heard the story.

"No. I was taken captive, and no one else knew where the stone was hidden." Beru seemed to be clearer on his story now.

"It must be what's calling you." Sade handed him a plate full of fish.

"If it is, we can use it to close the prison," Beru stated.

"How did the prison end up getting built if they didn't have the stone?" Astor asked the question the rest of us had heard the tales of.

"On the blood of others. Of a major sacrifice." Beru hung his head and dug into his food.

We grew quiet as we filled our bellies with fish. The day before, we'd fought, and this day, we had hope. We knew what we were looking for and Beru was getting his memory back. It would be no time until he realized he was the key.

“What tests were they doing?” Astor wanted to know when he finished his plate.

“Let the man eat.” Sade let out an exaggerated sigh.

“I don’t remember. I think I failed one. But I don’t remember what they were. It was physical, I’m sure.” Beru stared off into the distance.

“It’s okay if you don’t remember everything. It’s coming back.” I placed my hand on his arm, and he wrapped his fingers around it. I could feel Sade’s eyes on us. I was in for some questioning later when we were alone.

The rest of us finished our food, and we started to break down camp. I washed the dishes down by the water. Sade made her way next to me. She sat but didn’t offer to help clean. “So.” She rocked back and forth on her heels, her eyes dead set on me.

“What?” I looked back at her as I scrubbed a plate.

“Something’s going on.” Her eyes narrowed as she watched me. “Or something happened. I know you didn’t catch those fish.”

“You’re right. I didn’t.” I paid attention to the task at hand.

“He kissed you again, didn’t he?” She stopped rocking.

I scrubbed the dish and didn't answer her question. I wanted to tell her in my own time. I didn't want her thoughts to influence what I wanted to do. And anyway, she thought we would all die soon.

"You can't keep this from me. Let me live through you. That's why your face was so red this morning, wasn't it?" Her voice grew louder at her discovery. "And you baited me with food!"

I looked at her and smiled. She moved down, so she was beside me. "You cheeky girl. Now, go on. Tell me."

"There's nothing, really, to tell. He did kiss me, but it was quick. I went down, and he had already caught the fish." I kept my face toward the water, embarrassed at how I couldn't stop smiling.

"What was it like?" Sade nudged my arm and raised her eyebrows up and down.

I laughed out loud at her antics. "It was nice." I could feel my face starting to heat up again.

"What else? What did he say?"

"He wants us to go away when this is all over. To spend some time alone, but I don't know." I shook my head. I hadn't had time to think things over.

"I think you should. Besides, it will be good to have something to look forward too." Sade shrugged like it was no big deal to her.

"I'm done. We should get the boys moving. You know how slow they are." I stood up with the plates and began up the small hill. I balanced everything evenly, so nothing fell.

"Apparently, Beru is not slow." Sade ran past me.

I shook my head and laughed. Sade wasn't as predictable as I'd pegged her to be.

"It should be here," I told my crew as we entered what I thought would be the prison. I turned in a circle and looked around. Perplexed, I didn't recognize anything.

"I thought so too." Beru stepped out ahead of me and looked off into the distance. "The landscape is completely different."

"Is it because there is a rip? Maybe something happened in here to change that." Sade kept her fighting stance.

Iri appeared worried. "Is the wall completely down?"

"It could be." That was the worst-case scenario. I hoped we just had the wrong spot.

"We would know if the walls were down." Beru walked back to us. "Let's go ahead farther. It's around here somewhere."

"What should we look for?" Sade walked forward.

"You'll know when you see it," Beru called out to her.

Beru walked to the left as Sade, Iri, and Astor walked straight ahead. I hung back and followed Beru.

The land seemed familiar. The feeling was the same. Deep, dark coldness. It had to be around there somewhere. There were few trees or anything of a living nature, so it should be easy to see the buildings.

Beru walked up a hill and stood at the top. I waited for him to say something but lost my patience. “See anything?” I yelled at him.

“Nothing.” He ran back down the hill. “It’s familiar, though. It’s here.”

“I guess we have never been on this side of the wall,” I reminded him,

“That’s true. There must be an entrance somewhere.” Beru took off running, and I followed him. We could be chasing thoughts for hours. We had no idea what to look for and no idea if anyone could see us. There was nowhere to hide if we wanted to look for the entrance.

“It’s impossible.” I threw my arms up in the air. I expected to get there, find the rip, get the stone, fix the prison, and be on to my next life. I should have known it would not be that easy.

“Look for a ripple.” Beru ran back and forth in front of me.

I sighed. A ripple? That could take us months. The land was vast and barren, which made it hard to see anything. “There’s too much land to cover.”

“It’s around here somewhere. I know it is.” Beru kept running. “It’s close. I can feel it.”

I followed him and kept my eyes open for the ripple. I wasn’t sure what he meant, but he was being drawn to the stone. He had the most chance of finding it out of all of us.

“What if we don’t find it?” I called out to Beru, who was a short distance away from me.

Beru ran back to me. “What do you mean? That’s why we are here.”

I could tell I was testing his patience, but he was calm with me instead of yelling at me like I would have done to him.

“What do we do with it?” A million things ran through my head at the thought of collecting the stone. Things I hadn’t thought of before.

“We take it, of course. Figure out how we use it to keep the prisoners locked up.” Beru looked confused about my questioning, and I didn’t blame him.

“But you were supposed to take it to Onen Suun. He was going to use it to build the prison. What would he do now?" I questioned him hard. My own insecurities infiltrated my thoughts.

"We can worry about that when we have it. We are wasting time, Aria," Beru pleaded with me.

"We have no one to take it to," I yelled at him, not because I wanted to. I was unraveling at the thought of having the powerful stone in our possession.

Beru grabbed both of my shoulders and tried to calm me. "Let's just look for the opening. We don't even know if it's the stone that's pulling me here."

I nodded, aware of how ridiculous I was being. But something was nagging me on the inside. This may not be the best option. "Wait." I pulled Beru's sleeve as he tried to walk away from me to continue searching. He turned back to me and lowered his eyebrows. He didn't understand my reluctance. I stood opened-mouthed, unable to tell him my worries.

"Dreamwalk to Runa." Beru pulled me close. "Talk to her. Let me keep looking."

I nodded at his plan. Runa would know what to do with the stone. I watched as he walked off, and I began my descent into a dreamwalk.

It was easier than it had been in the past, perhaps because Runa left a channel open for me to communicate with her. It wasn't long before I was back in that white room that I disliked. Perhaps because I never got good news there.

"I've been waiting for you." Runa's back was to me. "I've been wondering what you are up to with those hoodlums."

"They are loyal friends. More like family." I wouldn't let her talk about them that way.

"Fine. Whatever they are. Just tell me what's going on." Runa sat down in her throne-like chair and offered me a downgraded version.

I wasn't sure how I should start the conversation. She hadn't exactly welcomed me there. "I need your opinion on what we should do."

"Have you gone south?" Runa settled in.

"Yes, they are looking for the entrance to the prison now."

"Then why are you here? Don't you want to be there when they find it?" Runa rang a bell and servants appeared with drinks for us.

"It may take some time. They are looking for a ripple in a very large space." I took a glass of what looked like red wine.

"I can't help with that." Runa waved her hand at me and shook her head.

“I don’t need your help with that. Could you just listen? I don’t have a lot of time.”

“Go ahead.” Her eyes narrowed.

She was interested. Otherwise, she would have thrown me out for talking to her like that. I had her in the palm of my hand, which worked in my favor. “Beru knows what he is being drawn to. It’s a stone Onen Suun tasked him to find.” I paused, half expecting her to stop me with more questions, but she sat still.

She offered me a fake smile. “I’m listening, as you wished.”

“It’s a stone called Death’s Breath.” No sooner had I said it, Runa’s smile disappeared, and she rose to sit on the edge of her seat.

“And does he have this stone?” Her voice was emotionless.

“No. It’s in the prison. He will know where to find it once we get in.”

“I see.” Runa looked off toward the side of the room and appeared to be deep in thought.

“You’ve heard of the stone?”

“Yes. I have.” Runa didn’t offer any more information.

“I need to know what to do once we get it. If it’s as powerful as Beru thinks it is, it’s not something I want to be carrying around with us.” I got up, unable to hold my energy together. If any lanterns or candles were near, I was certain I could light them just by looking at them.

“No, you’re right. It’s something you would want to keep hidden. Just not in the prison.” Runa stood up and walked over to the wall. She pressed some buttons, and her own personal bar opened. She poured two glasses of tan liquid. “Thinking of that stone makes me parched.” She handed me one of the glasses and I took it willingly.

“What should we do?” I was only too eager for her response. She knew more about the stone than perhaps all of us by the way she acted.

“Give it to Astor and Iri. Let them bring it to Western March. We can protect it here.” Runa sat back down on her throne.

“What will you do with it?”

Runa was a little too quick to ask to have it brought back there. She knew there would be a real danger in that.

“I’ll hide it.” Runa looked smug.

Her eagerness to take on such a power worried me, but I had no one else to trust. And frankly, I would be happy it would be nowhere near me.

"Then, you and Beru should leave and go far away. Stay away until we figure out the best way to handle the stone. The ur'gel will follow you, of course. It would help people in the Lower Forest as well. Give them time to build up what they lost."

I nodded, knowing she didn't mean anything by her comment, but it was a reminder of the pain and suffering I had caused to free Beru. "I see."

"Stay in the desert. It's far enough away." Runa gripped the throne's armrest.

"Okay. I'll do it." I wasn't sure what I had wanted her to say. I guess I expected something different. That I would be part of the plan to keep the stone safe. I wouldn't let my ego get the better of me.

"You can call on me if needed. Remember that." Runa nodded at me.

"Thank you." My voice was low. I should have been grateful for her help. I had sought her out. But something wasn't sitting right with me.

"Something's on your mind. You don't trust me, do you, Aria?" Runa leaned over and watched my eyes.

"I don't know who I can trust right now." I was honest. It wasn't necessarily her.

"We are dreamwalkers, you and me. We're on the same team."

"But you're above me. You know more than I do. You can do more things than dreamwalk," I countered.

"Yes, and so could you if you chose. I'm not holding you back. Now, of course, you are free to deal with the stone how you please. You can refuse my offer." Runa drank from her glass but didn't take her eyes off me.

"I accept your offer, and I do trust you. I wouldn't have come if I didn't." Mother Ofburg would not have come here if it wasn't safe. I had to remember that. "I trust you because of Mother Ofburg." I sat with my back straight, ready to return to my friends and look for the prison entrance.

Runa lowered her glass. "I take it you haven't heard, then."

"Heard what?" I was confused.

"Mother Ofburg has passed. Her body was found floating in the river." Runa's eyes filled with tears. "I thought you already knew."

I didn't move at first. Afraid if I did, what she told me would be true. I remained stiff as my cheeks began to spasm.

"I'm sorry to be the one to have to tell you. I can feel her in you. She gave you her energy?" Runa passed me a cloth to wipe away my tears.

"Yes." My voice was small. I broke out of my stiff trance and felt dizzy and weak.

"She knew what she was doing, then?"

"I believe so. I just didn't think it would happen so soon. I thought maybe I'd get a chance to say goodbye once this was all over." I wiped my eyes and Runa came over and sat on the arm of my chair. She pulled me toward her and wrapped her arms around me.

"We all go through things. Things we don't think we can live through. But we do. You're strong, Aria. You're young and have so much to learn. She'll live on through you." She kissed the top of my head.

"I can't imagine life without her," I muttered as I fell into deep sobs.

"She lives in you. She gave you her greatest gift. You have yet to discover it." Runa rocked me back and forth for a while. We said nothing.

When I was ready, I pulled away from her. "I'm ready to go back now."

"I know you are." Runa smiled and stood up. "I'm always close if you need me."

I nodded and gave my face one final wipe with the cloth. "I'm such a crybaby."

"You have a kind heart. A bad thing for a dreamwalker." Runa half smiled. "It's better to have a cold heart like mine." Runa sat back on her throne and wiped the lone tear that fell.

"I'll be back soon. With the stone. I'll trust you with it and do as you suggested."

"I'll be glad to see you when you do. Be careful—you never know who you can trust when that much power is at stake."

I drifted off into a dreamwalk, back to my friends, and thought about her last words. Could I trust Runa?

When I got back to the team, they were in the desert looking for the entrance to the prison. The wind was fierce and whipped the sand around, which cut into our skin. We climbed through the sand dunes and moved at a slow pace.

I used my shirt to cover my mouth and nose to prevent breathing in the sand, which only half worked. They had passed through the Blasted Lands without me and were more tired than I was. We needed to get to the Desert of Souls. Beru felt the pull of the stone bringing him there.

All we could see around us was desert, which was odd because it was ur'gel territory. It should have been filled with ur'gel that we had to fight our way through. Not that I was complaining. But something had to happen for them not to be there.

We carried on, one step at a time. It was hard work. In some places, the sand was up to our knees. We pulled each other through as we needed to.

I waved for everyone to come to me. Once they did, we all huddled into a circle, tightly squeezed together, and used our arms as a reinforcement.

“I need a break.” I panted. “How far away are we?”

“Not much longer. The winds will be much better once we make it over that hill,” Beru reassured us.

“Can everyone make it there?” Iri looked at our group.

We all nodded in agreement and stayed huddled together to take a much-needed rest.

“We need water.” Astor spit sand from his mouth.

“You won’t find it anywhere nearby.” Sade pulled out her flask. “Here. Take the last bit.”

Astor grabbed it before anyone could stop him and drank it back. “Thank you.” He passed the empty flask back to Sade.

“We can’t pass back through this. You’re sure this is the right way?”

“Yes. I can feel the pull stronger as we get closer to it. But I’m not sure how far away it is.”

“Where are all the ur’gel? Isn’t this place full of them? That’s what I always heard in Western March.” Iri shaded his eyes and gazed out toward the horizon.

I felt the world for Iri. He was practically bald. His scalp was raw from abrasions. The blood dripped into the sand as he stood in the same place. “Can you cover your head?”

"No use now. Are we ready to move? That hill is not that far."

We all nodded as we wrapped our mouths and noses the best that we could. Then we broke away and went as fast as we could to the hill. The more we moved, the farther it looked to be until we came upon it.

Beru was first. Once he saw we were close behind him, he jumped down and slid to the bottom. "No wind down here."

We all took the leap and slid down the hill. At the bottom, it was calm but still very hot and dry.

"This is so much better." Sade stood up first and wiped all the sand of herself the best she could.

"I'm stuck." Astor's legs were deep in the sand.

"Let's leave him here." Sade started to walk away but then turned around to smile at Astor, whose mouth had dropped open. "I'm just teasing."

I smiled at Sade and her inappropriate jokes. I dusted the sand off and watched as Beru headed out alone to scope out the land. For a moment, I wondered if he would sneak off and try to find the stone alone but then scolded myself for even thinking it.

I helped Sade and Iri dig Astor out and by the time we were done, Beru had reappeared.

"Desert of Souls is just over there." Beru sounded excited and ready to go.

"Let's get a rest before we go. My leg muscles are killing me." Sade began to flex as best she could in the sand.

Beru was just about to protest when I pulled him off to the side. I wanted to talk to him about the next leg of the journey. "I'm nervous about entering the Desert of Souls."

"Okay." Beru stood with his feet shoulder length apart and rubbed his chin with his hand. "What can I say to make that change?"

"You're not in the prison anymore. You can die now." I couldn't think of any other way to put it to him.

"I know. I'm going to be careful. Don't worry about that." Beru put his arms on my shoulders and leaned into me.

"I just wouldn't want that. I don't want you to die." I let him know how I felt, in case it was the last chance I had.

"And I don't want you to go anywhere, either." He smiled and leaned in to kiss me. I didn't care about the others seeing us.

"This isn't the end," I whispered as I hugged him.

"It's the beginning." He kissed the top of my head, and I pulled back and kissed him.

He looked surprised I would do that in front of the others, and so was I. I needed that kiss to get me through the next part.

Beru opened a pouch that hung from his hip. He took out a small coin and handed it to me. "This was from our first heist." He smiled. "Keep it on you for good luck. I don't need it anymore."

I held it in my palm, thankful to have a piece of him near me. I hadn't known he had kept it. My cheeks reddened at the thought. "Thank you."

He leaned in and kissed me again. I heard the others making gagging noises off to the side, so I knew it was time to break it up. We rejoined the group and started off in the direction Beru had scouted.

"It's not far. I could see it just over that hill." Beru pointed to a small hill that was close to us.

We pulled our feet through the sand and made it to the hill. The wind was bad, and we grimaced when we realized we would be back in it again.

"There's something sticking out of the sand." Iri pointed toward an object that looked like a peak. "Think that could be something?"

"Only way to know is to check it out." Beru went first. This time, we would have to walk downhill as the loose sand pelted us.

We held hands as we walked down. It was a smaller hill but hard to keep our footing when the sand moved under our feet. The dunes weren't packed tightly and made it hard to see. The sand whipped and cut our skin on top of the cuts we already had.

We finally made it down the hill, and the wind was worse. It was hard to breathe and there was nothing to hide behind. Sand packed my nose, and I tried to blow it out. My lungs were heavy. I was so done with the desert.

Iri grabbed my arm and moved me in another direction. I had started to wander off because it was hard to see where we were going. I held my head low and tried to keep track of Iri's feet in front of me, but it was hard to keep up with his longer stride.

I tried to look up to see where Beru was. To see if he'd made it to the object. But Iri blocked my view. I carried on, as difficult as it was. It seemed to let up a little bit, and I was able to see farther ahead of me. Sade and Beru had made it to the oddly shaped item. Iri was in front of me, with Astor by his side.

Without notice, I tumbled straight into Iri, who had stopped. "How are you doing?" He wrapped his arms around me so I could take a few full breaths.

"I've got this. Almost there, right?" I looked up at him. His entire face was covered in blood, but he never complained.

"Ready?" Iri mumbled through the top of my head.

I nodded and covered my face, and he began to walk again. I stayed close behind him and let him shelter the wind for me. I hung onto his shirt to guide me and walked faster. The wind calmed down as we got closer.

The thing was larger than we'd thought from far away. We were able to use it as shelter once we arrived.

"What is it?" I asked once I was out of the wind.

"It's a temple." Beru sounded excited. "But it's covered in sand. We will have to dig."

We formed a line and began digging around the object to first see where the door would be. We got on our knees and used our hands to pull the sand out. With each handful of sand we removed, half of it filled up again from the wind. We kept on, but no door was found.

My back started to hurt because of how long we had been trekking through the sand. I had sat back to stretch when I noticed I had hit a different pattern in the bricks.

"Hey! I think I found something," I called to the others.

They all got up and came over to where I was working. "Look at the change of pattern." I moved my hand over the difference. “Do you think this is the top of the door?”

“Let me see.” Beru gave me his hand and pulled me to my feet. “Iri, want to help?”

He nodded, and they both began pulling sand out much faster than I was doing it. It wasn’t long before the next row of brick was displayed, and it appeared to have wood under it.

“Is that a door?” Sade leaned in to get a better look.

“I think it could be.”

Iri and Beru widened their hole in the sand. They made it much larger, so if it was a door, we would be able to open it if it swung out. They pushed the sand hard and fast, with the motivation of getting inside the temple.

Sade, Astor, and I removed the sand they were pushing away so it would stop falling back into the hole. We kept up that momentum until they had uncovered the entire door. We all stood back and marveled at the ornate carvings on it.

“Well, are we just going to look at it?” Sade glared through the sand piled up in her eyes.

“Who should enter first?” Astor glanced around the group as well.

“Beru,” I nominated.

Iri seconded it.

"Go ahead." I gestured for him to open the door.

Beru stepped down into the hole, grabbed the metal circle, and pulled. The door didn't budge. He pulled harder the second time, and it still didn't open. He stepped back and tried to kick the door but only managed to hurt himself. He looked back up at us. "Iri? You want to open this?"

We all chuckled as Iri walked down and with one pull, the door opened. We stood back as if something would come out or be released. Beru stepped in first. We waited for him to tell us it was okay to enter, but he didn't come back out.

"Can you see him?" I called down to Iri,

"No. Its pitch dark." Iri lifted up his hands and then called, "Beru."

Silence. Iri called for him again, and he appeared at the door. "You won't believe this." He waved us to go down and enter the temple. Iri went first, then Astor and Sade, and I went in last.

It was pitch dark initially, but then the whole inner chamber lit up magically. It was hard to focus our eyes as we were used to the sand hitting our faces. There were many objects in the room but none that I recognized. Some looked to be gold or covered in gold. There were several barrels and boxes. Some items had blankets over them, and there was a door on the opposite side of the room.

“What is this place?” Astor reached out to touch the gold, but Beru grabbed him by the wrist.

“Don’t touch anything. It could be a trap. No one would leave this in the middle of nowhere without it being some kind of trap.”

“There could be food here. We have to have a look.” Astor pleaded with him and strategically walked in the opposite direction.

“Just don’t touch anything.” Beru was stern.

“I’m sure we are fine.” Astor grabbed a gold spoon off a box.

Iri grabbed Astor’s shirt and pulled him back, no sooner than a knife hit the floor where he had stood seconds earlier.

With Astor hauled off to the side, we all remained in our spots until Beru told us to move.

"I remember these things." Beru rubbed his head. "I can't think of from where."

"What do you remember?" I tried to talk him through it. He'd led us there for a reason. To find the random temple buried in the sand.

"That box. If you open it from the top, it will catch fire. You have to open it another way." Beru stepped around it and tried to look through the cracks. He pulled a lever and the boxed opened on the side.

I held my breath and waiting for something bad to happen, but nothing did.

"How did you know that was there?" Sade looked astonished.

"These were the tests. In order for me to have the stone, I had to do tests. It's all here." Beru spun around as he looked over everything in the room.

"Do you remember how to do them all?" It was over two hundred years since the last time he was there.

"I don't know." Beru examined all the items from a safe distance. "I remember this one. And this." He began to point out objects in the room.

"Does that mean the stone is in this room?" Iri sounded hopeful.

"It might be. We have to pass each test to find out." Beru started at the beginning of the room. "They went in order. The box was first and was the easiest to figure out."

"What one is next?" I looked around the room as if they would be numbered or something.

"The Barrel." Beru stood before it and scratched his head. "I don't remember this one quite as well.

"Take your time." Astor patted his back.

Beru shrugged Astor's hand off his back with a growl, startling Astor, who took a step backward and bumped into a crate. It fell to the ground.

None of us moved, barely breathing, waiting for the fire or knives to appear.

Nothing happened.

"Don't move. Just stand there and barely breathe," Beru snarled at Astor.

"What about the barrel?" I tried to get his focus back on solving the puzzles.

"It's not the top. It's one of the panels?"

"How do you know which one? They all look the same to me." Sade examined them.

"Look for a small number. It should be in black. A number two. There will be other numbers on it as well, though, so don't touch it until you are sure." Beru looked over the numbers and found the panel. "It's here."

"How do you open it?" Sade inspected the panel.

"I don't remember." Beru pushed a large gush of air out of his mouth as he struggled to figure it out.

"We need to stay calm and relaxed. We have as much time as we want." I tried to be the voice of reason.

Beru was normally calm. I didn't want him flipping out on this challenge.

"Stand back." He stood next to the barrel, placing his hand on the top of the numbered panel, and pushed. The barrel opened, and a small metal object appeared inside. He took it out with a steady hand.

"What is it?" I leaned in to inspect it.

"This will help us with our next puzzle. We need to find a green box. Don't touch it if you find it." Beru began to look for the box.

We all searched the room, leery of knocking over anything that could be deadly.

"I've got it," Sade called from the left side of the room. "It's under this yellow box."

"Don't move it," Beru yelled as he ran toward the box. "I know this one, and it needs to be done perfectly."

"Or what will happen?" I wasn't exactly sure I wanted to know.

"It will explode." Beru moved around the box. He found a spot to stick the metal object in, and the box opened.

"There's nothing inside this one." Astor leaned over to look inside.

"There isn't supposed to be."

"What should we look for?"

"I can't remember. It's red."

"This is red." Sade pointed to a small box under the table.

"So is this." I pointed to another small box that sat next to a cage. They were both red, and judging from Beru's face, he wasn't sure which was the right one.

"Which is it?" Iri asked.

"I don't know. But I have to pick one." Beru walked over to the one Sade found and picked it up. "Only one way to tell."Beru opened the box, and the ground began to move and shake. Beru closed the box quickly, but the ground kept moving.

"What does that mean?" I asked, looking at the others.

"It's the wrong box. Brace yourself." Beru tried to steady his feet as the ground gave way.

The lights flickered, and dust filled the chamber. The floor opened up at the same time Astor screamed, and he fell into the hole. Iri tried to grab him, but it happened too fast. We heard his body hit the bottom of the hole with a loud thud. The floor closed over him.

We were all in shock and couldn't believe what had just happened. We had lost our friend. Astor was gone because we got the puzzle wrong.

"Is he dead?" Sade held onto the wall.

"Yes." Iri began to cry.

My legs started to tremble and I got weak. My skin felt numb. I wasn't sure what to do or say to anyone. I didn't believe he had died when seconds ago he was there, making fun of Sade.

"We have to save him." Sade stared at the ground where the hole had just closed.

"He's gone, Sade. I watched him fall. He's gone." Iri's voice was low and soft.

I held my hand to my mouth to catch any sobs. I should have stopped it somehow. It shouldn't have happened.

"I'm sorry to say this, but we have to keep going. If we don't finish this puzzle in time, then we won't be leaving the temple." Beru looked defeated and ready to give in.

"What's next?" Iri wiped his tears. "No one else dies."

"Purple." Beru nodded. "It's a round purple basket."

"Do you have to get every one right?" Sade choked back her sobs.

"No, we just have to keep going." Beru looked at each one of us.

"Let's do this, then. For Astor." I declared.

We all looked for the purple basket, but we couldn't find it anywhere. We didn't want to move anything around, which made it more difficult.

"I've got it," Sade yelled. "Over here."

Beru walked over and picked up the basket. He flipped it around and pulled the handle off. Razer blades shot out from the wall and Sade and I both got sliced on our arms.

"Ow!" Sade covered her arm with her hand as blood ran down it.

My wound wasn't as bad, and I lost little blood. It was more like a scrape. The razers retracted into the walls just as quickly as they had appeared.

"Are you okay?" I walked over to Sade and looked at her wound. It was deep.

"I'm not sure. There's so much blood." Sade fell to the floor and banged her head.

"She's losing a lot of blood." Iri knelt next to her and tried to wake her up, but nothing he did worked. Iri turned to me. "Can you heal her, Aria?"

"We have to take her outside. I have no powers in here."

He picked her up, and we tried to head out.

"It's locked," Beru called out to us. "Once we start, we can't stop."

"Then let's get this done." Iri laid her down gently on the floor.

"What's next?" I was ready to end it.

"Yellow paper." Beru was already searching the room. "I've got it."

"Are you sure you have it?" Iri stayed by Sade's side.

"No. There are decoys. If this is right and I open it, another door should open."

"And if it's not the right one?" I wasn't sure I wanted to know. There was nothing he could do to stop it from happening to us.

Beru opened the envelope, and a door opened. We all breathed a sigh of relief that no one else got hurt.

"How many are left?" I looked at Sade, who desperately needed help. I wouldn't lose another friend. We had to get out of the temple, so I could close her wound quickly.

"Three more." Beru stepped into the next room.

"Stay with Sade." I motioned to Iri as I followed Beru into the other room. "What are we looking for?"

The door closed behind us.

"I forgot about that part. We need to find a blue pack."

They weren't hard to find. There were seven on the floor. They all looked the same.

"Ready? I'm just going to pick one." He pulled the top one off and a rock fell from the ceiling. He pushed me out of the way, and I fell on the other packs.

"That was too close." I picked myself up and looked at the rock that had almost killed me.

"I have to open another pack." Beru wrapped his arms around me. "I don't remember what happens if it's not right for this one, so stay alert."

Beru took his time and finally chose another blue pack. He opened it, and there was a key. He was able to unlock the door and get us out of the room.

“You both all right?” Iri’s worried voice was welcomed as we emerged from the room.

“We are fine,” I replied first. I didn’t want Beru to tell him what had nearly happened. He had enough on his plate to think about.

“Can we get out of here?” Iri had his hand over Sade’s wound.

“One more puzzle and the door should open. Orange box this time.”

We looked frantically for the box. I saw every other color but orange.

“It’s over here,” Iri shouted. The box was behind him and Sade. Beru rushed over to grab it and pulled the box down. He paused before he opened it.

“What should be in the box?” I leaned over his shoulder and waited for him to open it.

“A key. Is everyone ready?” Beru looked at Iri and then at me for confirmation before he opened the box.

We both nodded, ready for it to all be over. Beru opened the box. We all held our breath until we saw the key. “This should open something to get us the stone. Then the door will open, and we can get out of here.”

Beru, Iri, and I frantically searched the room for locks we could try the key in. We were careful not to move anything to set off another trap.

“This could be something.” Iri waved us over to a large chest.

Beru knelt and tried the lock. “It won’t turn. This isn’t it.” We went back to checking every box for a keyhole. We searched the room three times and were unable to find anything.

“We can’t give up. Sade is counting on us.” I paced the room. “Let’s each take a wall.”

Beru and Iri nodded, and we got back to work. I searched every side of every box until I found a keyhole. “I’ve got one!”

Beru rushed over and placed the key in the hole, and it turned. He pushed the top open, and there was the stone. He picked it up and held it for us to see. “Onen Suun thought this could save the world. It didn’t last time. Let’s hope it will this time.”

"You must leave her with me." I knelt next to Sade and started to heal her outside of the tomb. "The stone needs to go now." I didn't want to care about the stone, but I had to. We didn't lose Astor and almost kill Sade to let the stone get stolen. It was too powerful for us to handle ourselves; we didn't have an army to protect it. We weren't sure when we would be attacked.

Iri grumbled. He had lost Astor, and now Sade was not responding to my healing, and we were asking him to leave and go to Western March with the stone so Runa would protect it.

"Aria will look after her. They are like sisters." Beru tried to reassure him.

"I'm not sure I could handle anything happening to her." Iri wiped his eyes.

"I know how you feel." I stood up and hugged him. I feared for her life as well. Nothing I tried was working, and she had lost so much blood. "It's important Runa gets this stone. I only trust you. If it got into the wrong hands, it could be deadly." I stressed as much as I could without being insensitive.

"I'll do it. She wanted me to." Iri leaned over and kissed Sade's cheek.

Beru and I walked away to give him a moment with Sade.

"He lost Astor, and now I'm not sure about Sade." I tried my best not to cry. I didn't want Iri to see me. Beru wrapped his arms around me and held me tight.

I couldn't believe Astor was gone. My sweet, funny friend had died because I dragged him along on this journey and now Sade was close to death. I could lose two friends in one day.

"I'm ready now." Iri stood up. "Send word about her. Either way."

I ran to Iri and hugged him. He pulled back and patted my head. "I'll see you soon." Iri began his trek back to the Western March, leaving us in the desert.

"Is there anything I can get to help?" Beru knelt beside us. I laid my hands on her body and sent every ounce of energy I had to her wounds. Nothing worked. My thoughts went to Mother Ofburg. She had died in order to give us her healing energy and yet I had no idea how to use it or even find it within myself. She gave her life to the cause and now I may lose another life because I was unable to use her gift.

“I don’t understand.” I wiped the tears from my eyes as I leaned over Sade. “It’s not doing anything.”

“She’s your best friend. Is it because you’re too close?” Beru sat back to give me a room.

“Maybe, but I’ve healed people I know before.” I looked at her limp body. She was barely breathing.

“Can you use my energy?” Beru extended his hand.

I’d try anything. I took his hand and placed my other hand on her. I couldn’t pull any energy from Beru. I let go of his hand. I stood up and screamed as loudly as I could. My voice echoed around the barren desert. This wasn’t happening. This must all be a bad dream.

“Aria. You have this. You just need to focus.” Beru grabbed my arms hard and tried to pull me back together.

“I can’t do it. Something is wrong with me. Why can’t I save her?” I was frantic.

Beru shook me and then pulled me close to him. He held me as I cried. “I have to save her.”

Beru gently let me go and knelt to check on Sade. “She’s still with us but barely.” Beru reached for my hand. “We have to keep trying.”

"Yes." I wiped my nose on my sleeve and lay down beside her. I placed my hand on her stomach and laid my head next to her. "Sade? Can you hear me?"

Sade didn't move. Her skin had a bluish tint to it. I caressed her cheek as I watched her eyelids flutter. That gave me hope she was still there. Then I heard a gurgling sound coming from her chest.

"What's that noise?" Beru came closer.

"Her chest. It's not long now, my beautiful friend." I held back tears, and Sade looked toward me for the last time. She tried to talk but only made noises. "Shh. It's okay."

I held her in my arms and rocked her back and forth as her breathing became shallower. Beru stayed off to the side and gave me time alone with her. I could see the pain in his eyes as she took her last breath. I hung my head and sobbed as I continued to rock her back and forth in my arms. I didn't want to let her go. This shouldn't be her last day. I had lost too much and losing her was too much to bear. Sade, the great warrior, should not die like this.

I slipped into a trance, forgetting everything around me. I cried all my tears as I rocked her back and forth. I had forgotten Beru was still there.

"Aria. It's time, my love." Beru tried to take her from my arms, but I couldn't let him. I held on to her body and fought him off. He knelt and ran his hand over my head and down my back. “She isn’t here anymore. It’s okay to let her body go.”

I shook my head. “She comes with us.”

“We can’t carry her, Aria. We have to leave her here.” He tried to reason with me, but I wasn’t listening.

“There is a city. They bring people back from the dead. We can take her there, and they will fix this.” I pleaded with him.

He looked at me and then back at her. “We can’t take her body.”

He tried to touch me, but I pulled away from him. “I go where she goes. You can leave if you want.”

“I’m not leaving you in your grief. I have heard of the city you speak of.”

“You have?” I sat up straight, surprised he had heard of it. I wasn’t sure if it was real or just a story my father had read to me when I was a child.

“They don’t need her physical body. They need a treasured item.”

I searched her pockets and found the feather she always carried on her. “This was her father’s. He wore it in his headpiece.”

Beru took the feather from me. “This is all that we need, then.”

“You will take me there?” I questioned him. Begged him.

“If you want me to. I will. But you must be willing to give something to get her back. You won’t know what until they bring her back.”

“I’ll do it,” I said without hesitation. “I just want her back.”

Beru stood and left me alone with her to say my final goodbyes.

“I love you,” I whispered in her ear. I slowly stood, but almost fell over from the weakness in my knees.

“Are you ready?” He extended his hand to me.

“Yes.” I took his hand.

“Stay here. I’ll put her in the temple.” He waited for me to nod before he left.

I couldn't watch him pick her up and move her. I stayed outside with my back to the door. I closed my eyes and thought about when I would see her next. It wasn’t the end for her. She was a warrior and would come back. I’d make sure of that.

“What about Astor?”

“He’s in the temple somewhere. I don’t know where.”

I nodded that I understood. Such a strange way to die, I thought. I looked back at the temple where my two dearest friends lay and forced myself to leave with Beru. We needed to find someone to bring them back to us.

“We will find the city and bring her back. I only wish we could have helped Astor too.” We walked hand in hand over the sand dunes, ready to face whatever we had to for the sake of our friends.

The prison would have to wait until then.

Continue reading this series, Legends of the Fallen with book 4, Being the Suun

---

Grab the free prequel to the Legends of the Fallen series, Falling Suun here:

https://books2read.com/u/3R1ElD

Like the series Facebook page to stay up to date on all new releases

https://www.facebook.com/LegendsoftheFallen

Books by J.A. Culican

Novels

The Prince Returns-Keeper of Dragons book 1
The Elven Alliance-Keeper of Dragons book 2
The Mere Treaty-Keeper of Dragons book 3
The Crowns' Accord-Keeper of Dragons book 4

Second Sight-Hollows Ground book 1

Slayer-Dragon Tamer book 1
Warrior-Dragon Tamer book 2
Protector-Dragon Tamer book 3

Spark of War-Through the Ashes Prequel
Sword of Fire-Through the Ashes 1
Embers of Darkness-Through the Ashes 2
Blaze of Magic-Through the Ashes 3

Elemental Origin-Blood of Dragons Prequel
Fire Oath-Blood of Dragons 1

Short Stories

The Golden Dragon-Keeper of Dragons short story
Jericho-Keeper of Dragons short story
Phoenix-Hollows Ground short story
Savior-Dragon Tamer short story
Savior-Dragon Tamer short story

About J.A. Culican

J.A. Culican is a USA Today Bestselling author of the middle grade fantasy series Keeper of Dragons. Her first novel in the fictional series catapulted a trajectory of titles and awards, including top selling author on the USA Today bestsellers list and Amazon, and a rightfully earned spot as an international best seller. Additional accolades include Best Fantasy Book of 2016, Runner-up in Reality Bites Book Awards, and 1st place for Best Coming of Age Book from the Indie book Awards.

J.A. Culican holds a Master's degree in Special Education from Niagara University, in which she has been teaching special education for over 12 years. She is also the president of the autism awareness non-profit Puzzle Peace United. J.A. Culican resides in Southern New Jersey with her husband and four young children.

About H.M. Gooden

H. M. Gooden has been scribbling on everything since she first learned how to hold a pencil. While often told that her handwriting was atrocious, she persisted, and upon discovering computers and learning how to type, she realized that she was no longer limited by her (admittedly) messy writing.

Unfortunately, life and work and family have conspired to make it only possible to write in the wee hours or at coffee shops, so most of her love of reading and writing are indulged at times when only vampires and insomniacs abound.

Beginning in October of 2017, her love of writing and the characters in the world she has created burst into public view in her first book, Dream of Darkness, which follows the adventures of a group of girls fighting evil with abilities that H. M. Gooden would love to have.
As a result, 4 am has become even busier trying to find out what will happen to her paranormal buddies in the future, and book six, seven and eight are in the works.

Contact the Author

I can't wait to hear from you!

Email:
jaculican@gmail.com

Website:
http://jaculican.com

Facebook Author Page:
https://www.facebook.com/jaculican

Twitter:
https://twitter.com/jaculican

Instagram:
http://instagram.com/jaculican

Pinterest:
http://pinterest.com/jaculican

Add me on Goodreads here:
https://www.goodreads.com/author/show/15287808.J_A_Culican

Acknowledgements

Editor: Frankie Blooding
Cover Artist: Christian Bentulan
Formatting: Dragon Realm Press

www.ingramcontent.com/pod-product-compliance
Lightning Source LLC
Chambersburg PA
CBHW060550310726
48982CB00008B/1070/J

* 9 7 8 1 9 4 9 6 2 1 0 9 9 *